Also by
William Rubin:

Forbidden Birth

Forbidden Cure

To All Those
Who Have Lost a Loved One
Much Too Soon

FORBIDDEN BEGINNINGS

JACQUELINE'S TRAGEDY

WILLIAM RUBIN

A CHRIS RAVELLO MEDICAL THRILLER

Crystal Vision
Publishing

ISBN: 978-0-9975949-2-8
Copyright 2017 William Rubin
Printed in the US
All Rights Reserved
Published by Crystal Vision Publishing
Cover by William, Eilene, and Diane Rubin
Interior design by Christine Keleny: CKBooks Publishing.com
Proofreading by Anne Pottinger and Diana Delfino

Preface

Dear Readers,

Welcome to *FORBIDDEN BEGINNINGS: Jacqueline's Tragedy*. This book takes place prior to *FORBIDDEN BIRTH*, which has been on the Amazon Best Sellers lists for Medical Thrillers and Medical Fiction since January 2017.

Jacqueline's Tragedy chronicles the exploits of trauma surgeon Chris Ravello and was written for new and established readers alike. New readers will find it an entertaining introduction to the Chris Ravello Medical Thriller Series and a perfect lead-in to *FORBIDDEN BIRTH*. Established readers will enjoy learning more about Chris' backstory, including the life-altering events that occurred just prior to *FORBIDDEN BIRTH*.

Thank you for your support and happy reading!

Regards,
William Rubin

Prologue

The brutal images race through my mind. Blow after blow strikes her defenseless body. She tries in vain to fight back, to repel the attack. But the barrage is unrelenting. It pummels her face, head, and chest until finally, mercifully, she slips into unconsciousness. My hands clutch at my head. I'm ravaged with guilt and anguish. How could this have happened? Why wasn't I there to help her, to save her?

Oh God – not now.

The searing pain comes from nowhere. It rips through my chest, doubling me over as it races up my neck, down my arms, throughout my body. Don't think I can handle it much longer. My hands fly out in front of me, desperate to grab onto something, anything to brace my fall.

▷ Chapter 1 ◁

August 2014

"Thank God! The bullet's lodged in the cystic duct about a half inch from the gall bladder. A couple of inches in either direction and it would have torn through his liver, stomach, or intestines," I say as I peer past my blood-soaked gloves at the glistening projectile. "Nurse, give Doctor Peters two hemostats, and I'll take an Addison forceps."

"Right away, Doctor Ravello."

I look over at Peters, sizing him up. His blue eyes blaze with intensity, his brow is deeply furrowed. Good. Forty-four days into his surgical internship, this is the first of many bellwether moments for him. Five years earlier I stood where he is now. Two months ago, some forty-five hundred cases later, I finished up my chief residency in general surgery. Now I am the attending physician in charge - all the pressure falls on me. One false move on my part, one wrong step, and our patient will not see tomorrow. But wrong steps are for another day. Hardened by countless hours sewing together Harlem's more antisocial inhabitants, trauma surgery is an old friend of mine, and today I am up for all of my friend's challenges.

I reach in with my Addison forceps. "Clamp each side of the duct, Peters, and give me a clear field with that suction while I extract the bullet."

"Yes sir, right away."

Twenty-five minutes later we have the bullet out, the patient's cystic duct repaired, and his abdominal wall re-approximated with a series of absorbable and non-absorbable sutures.

"Good job, Peters," I say with a nod. "Your first of many traumas here at Washington General. You were well composed. Work on your suturing though, make it second nature. It will come in handy on the more challenging cases. Oh, and don't forget the damn paperwork – always plenty of that. I'll speak to the family."

"Sure thing, Doctor Ravello. Thank you," he says with a quick nod as if he's ready to salute me.

A wave of my hand activates the door sensor for OR 4. I stride down the hall, through double doors that lead to the ambulatory surgery recovery rooms. I find my patient's mother in bay four, just where I left her. Pulling down my mask I make steady eye contact with her.

"Mrs. Olivera, Derrick was very fortunate. The bullet missed his vital organs. The only thing that was hit was the duct leading to his gall bladder and we repaired that just fine. Things could have been much, much worse."

"Oh, thank God, doctor," Olivera says as she exhales in relief.

I place my hand on her shoulder. "I've seen Derrick before under similar circumstances, Mrs. Olivera. I know he's a good kid and just needs some more help finding his way. Please talk with one of our social workers, okay? They'll do what they can for both of you. Good luck."

"Thank you so much, doctor," she says through tearful eyes. "We will."

I smile back at Mrs. Olivera and hold onto her shoulder a few moments before heading off to see who else will need my help today.

❧ Chapter 2 ❧

"**H**oney, this is still like a dream," Michelle says with an infectious smile. It consumes her face as she stares out of our living room at the Long Island Sound.

My wife of ten years, love of my life since we met in our sophomore year at Fordham University, can hardly contain herself.

Neither can I.

"I know, baby. All those years of sacrifice, long hours, little pay…. We've finally made it!" I wrap my arm around Michelle's shoulders, snuggling my chest against her back, our bodies perfectly melded together. I tilt my head down so it touches the top of hers. "The water seems like it goes on forever out there even though the North Shore of Long Island is just a short boat ride away."

Michelle turns towards me, laughing. Even after all

these years together, her beautiful face, the wonderful way she carries herself, still leave me breathless. "You're starting to sound like our real estate agent, Doctor Ravello. What do you have to say about our in-ground pool or the beautiful bay windows we're looking through?"

"Just that they pale in comparison to your beauty, Mrs. Ravello," I say with sincerity.

"Awww, you always know just what to say to a girl." She winks at me. "You just might get lucky tonight, tiger."

Our lips meet and merge into one, just as our oldest, four-year-old Christine, ambles up. "Where's James, Mommy?"

Michelle pulls back, startled. "Uh, he's taking a nap, sweetheart."

"Oh. He sure sleeps a lot," Christine says with an innocent grin. Michelle smiles as she hoists her up, and we move through the living room, the dining room, and into the kitchen.

The kitchen, like everything else in our newly constructed house, is top of the line, no expense spared: white cabinets with beautifully etched glass faces reach to the ceiling; hand-painted backsplash tiles depicting playful scenes at the beach cover the area between the cabinets and our counter top.

"Are you getting hungry, kiddo? Maybe Mommy can work some of her magic and whip something up for you in our new kitchen."

I slide onto one of the chairs surrounding the center island as Michelle places Christine on the brown speckled granite countertop in front of me.

"How come you never cook, Daddy?" Christine says with a tilt of her head. She is my little darling, a beautiful amalgam of my and Michelle's best qualities and features. I melt every time I lay eyes on my daughter's doubly dimpled face – even when she is unwittingly putting me on the spot.

Michelle grabs eggs, bacon, and bread out of our Sub-Zero refrigerator and works her way over to the range, collecting a frying pan along the way.

"Christine, can you read this on the front of the oven?"

"Sure, Mommy. W-o-l-f. Wolf."

"Very good, sweetie. Now Daddy is a big, strong man as you know. He isn't afraid of anything in the whole wide world – except this wolf, it seems." Michelle's eyes lock on mine, a mischievous smile on her face. "I guess we have Grandma to blame for that one, huh? She always protected your daddy from big bad monsters – like the oven."

Christine's face scrunches up, her left eyebrow rising above the right as she struggles to discern what her mother means.

I tear my eyes away from Michelle and home in on Christine. "Er, how's preschool, kiddo?" I say with a sheepish grin.

"You're a silly daddy," she says with a chuckle. "There's no preschool during the summer."

"Of course." I stick out my tongue and cross my eyes. "How could Daddy be so silly? One thing I do know, Grandma and Grandpa will be over for dinner this Sunday."

"Yeaaahh!" she says with a little dance and wave of her hands. "I can show them our new house and ask Grandma how she kept you safe from the monsters. Maybe James will be up from his nap by then," Christine says with an authoritative look on her face and a quick nod.

▷ Chapter 3 ◁

Stab wounds litter our patient's chest. Hank, a cabbie who normally works the Upper East Side, wandered too far north this morning in search of a fare and paid the price for his indiscretion. A lacerated right lung allows air to leak out into his chest cavity. Each breath he takes fills his right chest cavity but not his lung. Eventually, the air will compress his lung, pushing it across his body, where it will drive his heart into cardiac arrest.

Peters and I move quickly to open up Hank's chest and repair his laceration.

"BP is 70 over 40 and his heart rate is becoming irregular. We're losing him, Chris," yells Dr. Craig Chang as he injects more meds into Hank's IV.

"We're moving as fast as we can. I think he's bleeding into his pericardium. How much time do we have, Craig?"

"A minute tops...maybe less."

"Shit! No time to crack his chest. Nurse, give Peters the ultrasound probe. I'll take an inch and a half long 18 gauge spinal needle on a 60 ml syringe."

"Peters, hold the probe at the bottom of the sternum, just below the xiphoid process. Show me the blood in the pericardial space."

"Chris, he's in arrest! I'm pushing meds, but we're losing him!"

"Nurse, quickly, a number 11 blade. I'm going in just above the fifth rib."

I puncture the skin with my scalpel, then slowly advance the needle, aiming towards our patient's left shoulder while I pull back on the syringe's plunger.

Peters, Chang, and the nurse look on, transfixed. The cabbie's EKG continues to flat-line despite our best efforts. Beads of sweat dot my forehead and face.

Seconds seem like minutes, then I feel it. An almost imperceptible pop as red fluid rushes into my syringe. We're in! One milliliter, then five, then ten races into the empty space. The EKG dances to life and assumes a regular rhythm. Peters, Chang, and the nurse collectively exhale.

Our patient is far from okay, but now we have a fighting chance to save him.

Over the next hour and a half, we continue our grueling work, methodically isolating and repairing each wound in our cabby's heart, lung, and chest cavity.

When it is all over, our patient's chest and abdomen look like a battlefield – but at least he's alive.

In the doctor's lounge, slumping forward, head in my hand, I am drained but deeply satisfied. It took every bit of knowledge, training, dexterity, and skill I possess, but none of that matters. What's important is I found my way through it and helped another patient cheat death in the process.

⟩ Chapter 4 ⟨

Sunday afternoon at the Ravello residence in beautiful Rye, New York – it's the best time of the week. Jacqueline and Bill Ravello, aka Mom and Dad/ Grandma and Grandpa, are over for our weekly family dinner. My best friend, Kevin Kennedy, is here as well. He is like a brother to me. Michelle, Christine, James, and I round out the crew. Our magnificent seven use this time to catch up with each other and enjoy some great cooking courtesy of Mom and Michelle. Today is extra special, as it's the first time Michelle and I are hosting the event at our new home, a four thousand square foot, five bedroom Victorian in one of Westchester County's more exclusive neighborhoods.

Michelle gathers the children at the top of our sprawling staircase, putting the finishing touches on their hair, as the rest of us catch up with each other in the living room.

Dad, a retired NYPD detective, who worked many of those years in the Bronx, and Kevin, a detective first grade stationed at the 17th precinct in Midtown Manhattan, trade war stories. The two have known each other since Kev and I met in fourth grade. His family had just moved to Ossining from Queens, mine from the Arthur Avenue section of the Bronx, better known as Little Italy.

"So I'm investigating a robbery on 181st Street and Hughes Avenue. I'm still wet behind the ears, trying to make a name for myself as a detective third grade," my dad says, leaning in. "I find this low-level mobster, Jimmy 'No Nose' Ciachi, in deep with the Godfather's wife! He about has a heart attack when I bust in and see him plowing her on the couch, his sweaty red face all contorted like a pretzel. Next thing you know I cut a deal with Jimmy to keep the whole thing under wraps in exchange for him becoming an informant." Dad slaps Kennedy on one of his massive shoulders. "Ended up making detective first grade off of all the busts from the intel Jimmy gave me!"

Kennedy bellows with laughter, his huge chest straining against the bright blue Polo shirt he is wearing.

"Ah, you've got the best stories, Bill! Most of my busts these days are drug related, low-level stuff. Turf war skirmishes, crimes committed to get money for drugs. You know, that kind of shit." A wistful look takes over Kennedy's face. "I'd love more interesting action."

14

Kennedy stands well over six feet tall, broad-shouldered, ruggedly good looking. Most people know him superficially. To them, he is a living monument of muscle, determination, and grit, the physical embodiment of an immovable object and an irresistible force rolled into one. But we who know him best, know him as so much more. He remains, in the best of ways, the same scrappy, vulnerable little boy I met in fourth grade. That pre-Goliath version of Kennedy still resonates in him today: big-hearted, idealistic, and selfless. He ambles over to me, the floor of our living room quaking under him. He drapes his left arm over my shoulder, his right arm tussling my hair as he addresses my mother.

"Ya done good with this one, Jackie. Summa cum laude at Fordham, Class of 2005, tops in his med school class at Stony Brook, one helluva surgeon at the busiest trauma center in the city. No wonder he's got this frigging picture-perfect estate overlooking the water." He looks me up and down and continues with a sarcastic smile, "Lord knows how you pulled it off with so little to work with, but you did."

Ma's eyes reach towards the heavens as a small smirk appears. She winks at Kennedy. "You didn't turn out too badly yourself, Detective. Now, why don't you give an old lady a hug and then gather everyone up for Chris' magic show."

Kennedy complies, capping the moment with a

salute and an "Aye, aye, ma'am." She waves her head in mock frustration and chuckles at the behemoth, then turns to me, her hands resting on the sides of my upper arms.

"I'm so proud of you, Christopher. This new house, your career, the two wonderful children you and Michelle are raising.... I always knew you could do it." Mom beams with pride.

Blushing, I try to downplay it. "I'm as surprised as anyone, Ma, with how well it's turned out. For a lot of years, I was a major screw up. You were the one who pulled me through all the fights, the turmoil, the feeling I didn't fit in when we moved to Ossining from Arthur Avenue." A smile fills my face. "I don't know how you hung in there with me, Ma, how you believed in me when I didn't even believe in myself. You made this all possible. Thank you so much."

Tears rim my eyes. Mom's mist up as well.

"Oh Christopher," she says as we lean into each other and hug. "Can you come to the kitchen with me? I have something for you in my purse."

"Sure, Ma. Lead the way."

Mom glides through the dining room and into the kitchen, checking on the meal she and Michelle have prepared. The aroma of lasagna and garlic bread in the oven waft through the air, bringing me back to happy Sundays from my childhood. Mom stirs the mac and cheese she is making for the kids, adding in seasoning as she goes. Sipping a glass of cabernet sauvignon, I admire her, reflecting on how lucky I am to have such a wonderful woman as my mother. Many are not so fortunate.

"I meant what I said a moment ago, Ma. I felt so lost, like such an outsider once we moved to Ossining." I stare down at my glass, place it next to her beige purse on the counter top. "There were plenty of kids at Park School determined to make me feel that way, plenty of fights to be had. But you were always there for me, carrying me when I was lost, mending my wounds, defending me with my teachers and the principal." My admiration spills over. "You were my champion, my hero, every step of the way. How did you always know the right thing to say or do?"

Mom's rosy cheeks swell. "Oh Christopher, it's not hard when you love your child as much as I love you." She laughs. "We certainly had our trials, didn't we? But I wouldn't change a moment of it. Do you remember that fight you got into in seventh grade, a few years after we moved?"

"How could I forget?! Three years in Ossining and kids were still giving me grief." I shake my head. "That time it was Mark Petrobono and three other kids. They worked me over pretty good, but I held my own, breaking one kid's nose, another's pinky, and giving the other two black eyes. It was that fight that finally got me some respect, got those guys off of my back."

"That's not the part I remember most. It was the part that made my heart ache for you but also filled me with pride and joy. That fight made me realize how strong and special, how determined my boy was. Do you remember why you fought them?"

My face flushes with anger as I recall the words. "They called you a Bronx Guinea Hag, said none of us belonged with them, that we should just go back to where we came from." I smile with pride as I recall the details. "You told me you didn't want me getting hurt on your account, but I told you I could take care of myself, that nobody was going to get away with calling my mom names."

Mom's smile is filled with joy and wisdom. "Four boys against one, and you got the better of them. I know I was supposed to act appalled at you fighting, that as your mother I should have told you it was wrong. But I grew up in the Bronx." She winks at me. "I knew what a struggle life was." Pride fills her face again. "That moment I knew with certainty, no matter what obstacles life threw your way, you would tackle them head on and overcome them."

Mom and I embrace for a moment. She leans back and pulls a tissue from her purse and dabs at her eyes.

"Ma, are you okay?"

"Yes, I'm fine dear. I just want you to know how proud I am of you. Seeing what you've accomplished, what a wonderful life you and Michelle have built for yourselves...." Mom smiles broadly through her tears. "I'm glad you found a strong woman, Christopher. A mother's always concerned about who her son will marry, who will take care of him when he leaves home. You and Michelle will pull each other through the darkest hours of your lives long after I'm gone. If I had to die now, I'd die happy, knowing how wonderfully my little boy has turned out."

I kiss Mom on the forehead and hug her. "Hey, Mom, don't get all melodramatic and serious on me now, huh? You're not going anywhere for a long time." I chuckle. "You've got two beautiful grandchildren counting on you to spoil them."

Mom dries her tears as she speaks. "Sorry for going a bit overboard, but what can you expect from a mother? Here, I got something for you." Mom reaches into the depths of her purse and pulls out a sturdy white box with a bright blue bow. It envelopes her hands. "Here, open it."

"Uh, okay. What's this all about?"

Mom's face fills with anticipation as I untie the bow and open the box. A puzzled look comes over me as I stare at the large gold medallion. It depicts a man, a club in his hand, fire around his head. The medallion is thick, filling my hand with its size and weight as I lift it and the chain it is on out of its box. "It's beautiful, Ma. But what's with the flame around the guy's head?" I smirk at her. "Are you trying to remind me not to be a hot head?"

Mom gives me the look reserved for mothers when their children misbehave. "Very funny." She grabs the gift from me. "It's a St. Jude medallion, Christopher. He's the patron saint of lost or hopeless causes. His feast day, October 28th, happens to be your birthday."

My look of confusion speaks volumes.

"You wear this as a reminder, dear." Mom's knowledge of Catholic saints is encyclopedic. Mine not so much.

"A reminder of what?"

"To always do good in the world, to help and protect those in need, no matter how lost they are or how hopeless their cause seems to be. Do this and St. Jude and I will always be there to watch over and protect you."

I'm touched by Mom's thoughtfulness. I undo the clasp and slide the chain around my neck, the hefty medal coming to rest on the center of my chest. I lean over and kiss her. "Thanks, Ma. I'll wear it with pride and do my best to live up to its meaning."

"I know you will."

"We better get back out there before everyone else thinks we took off with the food," I tease.

Mom smiles, then leads the charge back to the living room, filling the air with her joyfulness. "Where are those precious grandchildren of mine? You're going to be seeing a lot of Grandma and Grandpa while Mommy and Daddy celebrate their big tenth anniversary in Australia."

§

Donning my magician's hat and my favorite navy blazer, I tap my magic wand on the living room table. The kids look on, mesmerized, as they sit on Michelle's lap, one on each knee, on the plush couch. Mom and Dad are at Michelle's side. Kennedy fills a sturdy seat next to them, ready to take in his first Ravello magic show.

Over the next ten minutes, I amaze Christine and James with my card tricks and sleight of hand. Objects appear and disappear in my right hand as if out of thin air. I take an appreciative bow and receive well-earned hugs from my children before they scamper off to the dining room table with their mom and grandparents.

Kennedy lingers as I flip over my top hat, placing my wand and paraphernalia inside, and peel off the sports jacket. "Nice work, buddy. The kids were really eating it up." He reaches for the right arm of my blazer. "Guess the jacket has a compartment up the sleeve where you store stuff, huh?" I pull the jacket back, a stern look taking over my face. Shooing him towards the dining room, I chastise him. "Some things are better left unsaid."

He playfully admonishes me in return. "Geez, all right already, Houdini. It's not like we're dealing with life or death here. Can't blame a guy for just being curious."

▷ Chapter 5 ◁

Five days ago Michelle and I set down in Sydney, Australia at 8:47 a.m. local time, exhausted from our twenty-three hours of traveling but ecstatic to be exploring the "Down Under." It's been a whirlwind ever since.

"Sweetie, you're like the Energizer Bunny, just a little taller and not quite as furry," I say with a laugh. "Who'd have thought with a sixteen hour time difference, that in the first four days we would see Sydney Harbor, enjoy a performance of Don Giovanni at the Sydney Opera House, go on the Royal Botanic Gardens walk, visit The Rocks, take the Manly Ferry, visit Darling Harbor, and take in the Queen Victoria Building and Art Gallery of New South Wales and the Chinese Garden of Friendship. If I didn't know better, I'd say you've been popping amphetamines when I wasn't looking," I say with an amused smile.

"Life's too short, honey, and what's a few greenies between friends?" the love of my life replies with a chuckle. Her eyes dance with energy and vitality as her raven hair swirls in the wind. "I want to soak in as much as we can. Who knows if we'll ever take a trip like this again?"

I come up to Michelle and rest my hands on her shoulders. I peer down at my wife, the woman with whom I have shared so many of life's trials, tribulations, and triumphs. The woman who singlehandedly kept us afloat financially, working as a pharmaceutical sales rep during my time in medical school and as an intern. Only the demands of motherhood pried her from her role as breadwinner, and even then only after my crazy life as a surgical resident dictated we make the change.

A broad smile fills my face. "We've made it through all the crazy struggles in our life, baby. Working like a dog at Fordham University to get into med school. Four insane years there, praying I got into a good surgical residency while you worked your tail off at Agile Pharmaceuticals. Five exhausting years, working ninety hours a week training at Washington General while we started a family. We've paid our dues, big time, Michelle. Get used to these kind of trips. It's nothing but clear sailing for us from now on."

§

"Bill, I'm going to head to mass now at Our Lady of Mount Carmel and help Father Domico out at the soup kitchen before I get some things for dinner. Are you okay with Christine and James for a few hours?" Jacqueline calls out, worry written across her face.

"I've got everything under control, Jackie," Bill replies with bravado, as James flings a spoonful of strawberry oatmeal onto his grandfather's face.

"I can see that," Jacqueline chuckles as she walks into the kitchen. "Thirty years on NYPD, the last twenty as a homicide detective first grade, you should be able to handle a two- and three-year-old for a few hours." Jacqueline gazes upward before crossing herself.

Christine howls with delight before regaining her composure. "Are you okay, Grandpa?" A few more giggles break through as Christine reaches out with a napkin to clean off his face.

"So why am I so worried this will be a total disaster?" Taking a deep breath she continues, "Maybe I should just stay home."

"Not on your life, my dear wife," he sings in reply, doing his best Frank Sinatra imitation. "I know how you love making the trip down to Arthur Avenue and going to mass down there. You deserve a little outing, so scoot," Bill says with a brush of his hands as Christine wipes oatmeal off his face.

Jacqueline laughs at the sight before her. "I'm not sure that's a good idea. What about Christine and James? Who will–"

"We'll all be fine. Now go on, shoo, but uh, be sure and add strawberry oatmeal to the market list."

Jacqueline sighs before leaning down and kissing Christine, then James. "Grandma will bring you back that Italian nougat candy you love so much from Gino's Pastry Shop, and then you can help me make dinner. If you're good while I'm gone, we can make a surprise for dessert. Doesn't that sound nice?" Jacqueline says, trying hard to convince herself everything will be okay. She looks skeptically at Bill before turning back to her grandchildren. "Take good care of Grandpa. We don't want any visits from the police while I'm gone," Jacqueline quips with mock horror before pecking Bill on the cheek and slipping away.

§

Finally a respite from the breakneck sightseeing of earlier in the day. Michelle had planned this romantic dinner exactly one month ago. Tetsuya's opens at 5:00 p.m. daily and within thirty minutes books all of its reservations for exactly one month later. Michelle is a major foodie and has been dying to try this place for years, so here we are.

"So, was it worth it, Mrs. Ravello, staying up till one a.m. a month ago so you could snag us this reservation?"

"Definitely! This place is amazing! I love the cute

Japanese garden and this French-Asian tasting menu is out of this world. Besides, it gives me a glimpse into the crazy hours you keep, Doctor Ravello. As I recall, that night you were piecing together a couple members of the Harlem Hoods, who were on the wrong side of a turf war with the Bloods."

I reach across the table and take Michelle's hand in mine. "Honey, I couldn't have asked for any better partner in all of this. I don't know what I'd do without you."

"Aww, thanks, sweetie. I feel the same way," Michelle replies with a sensual smile. "I'm loving this new phase in our lives. What should we order for dessert?"

§

Jacqueline loves being tethered to the old neighborhood where they raised Chris from birth until age seven and Emily until she was fifteen. They lived in a small apartment, just north of the Arthur Avenue indoor market, next to and above Teitel Brother's. They didn't have much money in those days, but happiness was ever abundant – at least as far as Chris, she, and Bill were concerned.

Chris' wayward sister, Emily, was a completely different story.

Jackie never wanted to leave this neighborhood, but Bill was right. Ossining was a much better place for Chris and Emily to grow up, despite all the hazing Chris endured after the move. Jackie wished she had been more receptive when Bill first brought up the idea of the move. Her fierce opposition delayed them, with disastrous consequences for her family. Jackie bows her head and lets out a deep sigh as she walks along the crowded street. Despite the intensity of the summer sun beating down on her, a chill runs through her. She would never forgive herself for her poor judgment. If they had moved sooner, all the heartache with Emily might have been avoided. She might still be a part of their lives today.

Emily was eight years older than Chris. It was her falling in with the wrong crowd in the neighborhood that prompted Bill to push for the family's move. Tears come to Jackie's eyes as she thinks of her poor daughter. Sixteen years since her disappearance and the pain still sears during moments such as these. She dabs at her eyes with a tissue and shudders. As a young girl, Emily was soft spoken and painfully introverted, despite Jackie's attempts to draw her out of her shell. She had few friends. Her only interests were reading, particularly the poems of her namesake, Emily Dickinson, and perfecting her charcoal drawings of life in the Bronx.

Emily spent long hours locked in her room in sullen isolation, these two activities her only outlets. Jaqueline clutches at her chest now as she halts her walking, the reminiscences overpowering her. When Emily turned fourteen everything fell apart. She began to cut class, dress Goth, pierce her nose and eyebrows, and talk back to Jackie and Bill with increasing frequency and intensity. Jackie shakes her head now, recalling how she foolishly dismissed it all as a phase of early adolescence. But Bill knew better. He kept a close eye on their daughter and her newfound friends and tried, unsuccessfully, to drive away the more noxious ones. Just after Emily's fifteenth birthday, Bill found a few marijuana joints laced with PCP in her room. It was the final straw. The Ravellos moved to Ossining two weeks later, in time to save Chris from the ravages of their once-beloved neighborhood, but not Emily.

After the move, Emily continued to act out and make poor choices. Several attempts at drug rehab failed. Pregnancy at age eighteen lead to an ill-conceived, tumultuous marriage to her then boyfriend, Jeff. The two stayed together, even after Emily's miscarriage, until their disappearance on New Year's Day in 1998. Months and months of searching, hoping, and torment ended in futility. They never learned if Emily abandoned them, was kidnapped, or killed. Only by the grace of God and with her husband's and son's unwavering love and support, was Jackie able to survive the ordeal.

Jackie looks around at the buildings, the streets she used to call home. The neighborhood has deteriorated steadily these last twenty-five years. A few pockets of safety, of warmth, remain: the church, the indoor market, and Borgatti's pasta shop. Truth be told, Jacqueline feels uneasy walking around much of the area now, but what can she do? She can't turn her back on the parish she has known and loved for so many years. Besides, they need her, and she needs them.

§

Father Domico approaches Jackie just after mass at Our Lady of Mount Carmel. "Good to see you, Jacqueline. How is your family?"

"Everyone's doing great, Father. We're watching Christine and James for a couple of weeks while my son and Michelle celebrate their tenth wedding anniversary with a trip to Australia."

"Splendid! What a great way to mark a decade together." The priest's voice becomes wistful. "We're getting old Jacqueline. Has it really been ten years since I married Chris and Michelle here?"

"Yes, it has. But don't worry, Father, we both still have a lot of life left in us," Jacqueline says with sincerity.

"Of course, of course we do. So, I'll see you in a few hours at the soup kitchen?"

"Definitely. I have a little food shopping to do and am going to try and squeeze in a quick trip to the botanical gardens, but I'll be back in plenty of time to help serve lunch, Father."

The priest shakes her hand. "Great, I'll see you a little later then." He turns to walk away, then pauses and turns back. "I wish more parishioners shared your passion for life and love of service to others, Jaqueline. Say hi to Josephine at Borgatti's for me."

Jacqueline, embarrassed by the compliment, blushes and looks down before composing herself and raising her gaze. "You're too kind, Father. I'll let Josephine know you were asking for her."

§

Michelle's head lays on my chest, our bodies cooling down under the sheets after the fervor of making love. "Oh, baby, I love you so much. These last five days have been magical. If it's all a dream, don't wake me up." Michelle leans up and kisses me before returning her head to my chest.

I smile, my eyes misting up. "These are the happiest moments, the best days I've ever known, my love." I cradle Michelle's head and sigh. "It would take a herd of wild elephants to rouse us from this bliss."

§

Jacqueline glances down at her watch. She slips prosciutto, the lamb tenderloin, and an assortment of cheeses next to the ravioli, filling the cooler to the brim. She places the cooler on the floor of the front passenger's seat in her Buick LeSabre and wedges it between two bags. The Torrone nougat candy, strawberry oatmeal, and two small hand puppets – a zebra for James and a pony for Christine – sit in one of the bags. The second bag contains sugar, vanilla extract, all-purpose flour, and unsweetened baking chocolate to make brownies later on with the kids. Jackie still has an hour before she needs to be back at Our Lady of Mount Carmel. Just enough time to sneak a peek at the rose garden, which is so beautiful this time of year.

Jacqueline fidgets in the driver's seat. She hopes Bill is doing all right with Christine and James. He has about as much experience being alone, caring for young children, as she does firing her husband's .38 caliber special, which is, of course, none. She should call and see how they're doing. But would Bill's feelings be hurt by her checking up on them? Jacqueline pulls out her phone as she ponders what to do. A carefully worded text wouldn't be seen as checking up on him and would accomplish the same thing, she reasons. She types away, adding emoticons at the end. She stares at the message, rereading it. *Hmmm, that should be okay, no?* A car's blaring horn snaps her to attention. The driver gesticulates at her to pull out so he can grab her space. Jackie sighs. The text will have to wait. Jacqueline tosses the phone down on the seat next to her and pulls out into traffic.

A few turns later and she is on Southern Boulevard, sandwiched between Fordham University on the left and the Bronx Botanical Gardens to the right. A man standing near his car, waving his arms for her to pull over, catches Jackie's attention. That's all she needs right now is another impatient Bronx motorist. Honestly, hasn't he heard of AAA or seen the Mobil station just a short walk away? Surely he can get help there for whatever ails his vehicle. As Jackie slowly drives by she is torn; she wants to help, but she doesn't know the first thing about cars. What use could she be to the man?

Then she sees it. Another man lying on the sidewalk next to the car, his white t-shirt stained red.

A trained RN, Jackie jars the car to a stop. Her purse and phone fly forward off the seat, the oatmeal, nougat candy, and hand puppets scatter on the floor. She runs out of the car towards the injured man. As Jackie reaches the supine man and kneels down to assess his injuries, the other man circles behind her, glad she has stopped to help. His left arm is a blur, but Jackie senses something and shifts quickly. The blunt object, destined for the center of her skull, crashes down just above her right earlobe instead.

Dazed, Jackie tries to pull away, but the men pounce on her like predators battling for a kill. She bites one man's forearm as he wraps it around her waist. Jackie tears at the other man's face as he lunges forward to subdue her. He screams as her long nails rip flesh from his left cheek and stab at his eye. Jackie battles fiercely, kicking, screaming, and jabbing at the assailants, but it only delays the inevitable. They pound her face with a barrage of fists and feet, determined to subdue her at all costs.

"We gotta get the hell out of here, this woman's unbelievable."

"Huh? What about the purse. We should get that out of her car, make it look like a robbery gone wrong."

"Just leave the friggin thing. With all the commotion she caused, the cops'll be here any minute."

As if prophetic, sirens sound off in the distance, gaining in intensity as the police hurtle towards the assailants.

"Shit! Run!"

§

I jolt forward in bed, scrambling towards the ringing phone. The blood drains from my face as I listen. "Holy shit! Is she okay? How did it happen?" I scream.

Dad, in a lifeless voice replies, "We don't know much right now, Son, just that your mother was found badly beaten, lying on the street by the botanical gardens. She's in surgery at Jacobi Medical Center. We're heading there right now."

My brain is a whirl of thoughts and confusion. This can't be happening! Of all the people to attack, someone had to pick Ma? She'd never hurt anybody. Hell, her life is about *helping* others. She's the most selfless person we know.

I look over at the clock on the nightstand and force myself to think in straight lines. "It's four a.m. here, Dad. Michelle and I are in Sydney. We'll catch the first flight back home. I'll let you know the details once we figure them out. Let me know more once you see Ma. "

"Okay. I love you, Son. We'll see you both soon."

"Love you too, Dad. Bye."

Michelle's face is overcome with anguish. "What happened to Ma, Chris?" she says tentatively, the sheets pulled up almost to her face as she awaits my reply.

"Somebody attacked her near the Bronx Botanical Gardens. She's in surgery at Jacobi."

Michelle's face collapses, covered in tears. She lunges forward and embraces me. "Oh my God! Oh my God!"

Ma is the lifeblood of our family. Dad's wife for nearly forty years. My rock and savior through a turbulent childhood and my troubled early adult years. She is like a mother to Kennedy and Michelle too, pulling them through tragedies that would have buried most people. And now she is badly beaten, no doubt fighting for her life, the victim of some sick person's plans.

Oh God, I can't comprehend it, can't fathom life without Ma. My despair is deep and dark, seemingly endless. Anxiety tears through me. Michelle and I have to get back there in time, have to help her pull through this.

▷ Chapter 6 ◁

The brutal images race through my mind. Blow after blow strikes her defenseless body. She tries in vain to fight back, to repel the attack. But the barrage is unrelenting. It pummels her face, head, and chest until finally, mercifully, she slips into unconsciousness. My hands clutch at my head. I'm ravaged with guilt and anguish. How could this have happened? Why wasn't I there to help her, to save her?

Oh God – not now.

The searing pain comes from nowhere. It rips through my chest, doubling me over as it races up my neck, down my arms, throughout my body. Don't think I can handle it much longer. My hands fly out in front of me, desperate to grab onto something, anything to brace my fall.

A stewardess hears the commotion, my body bouncing off the sink, slumping against the door. She calls to me and knocks on the door, gently at first, then louder, insistent. A moment later she has the door open and I come crashing down on her. By now, Michelle hears the uproar, the shrieks of nearby passengers, and rushes to my aid.

"Oh my God! Chris, what's happening?"

I look up at my wife, through barely open eyes, my clothes and face drenched in sweat. I struggle to get the words out before I give in to unconsciousness. "An attack...so painful."

§

The stewardess comes by again. She looks at me, her voice filled with concern. "Are you okay, Doctor Ravello? Is there anything we can get you?"

Through weary eyes and a weak smile, I reply, "I'm fine now. Thank you very much for your help."

The stewardess addresses Michelle. "We should be landing at JFK soon. Let me know if you need anything else."

Michelle smiles back and her. "I will. Thank you for everything, Tammy. I think we're okay for now."

As Tammy heads away, I turn to Michelle. "How embarrassing, a full blown attack on a crowded international flight. I'm so sorry for the trouble, baby."

"Chris, don't be silly. I'm just glad you're all right. Is everything really back to normal?"

"Yeah, I'm fine." I rub the side of my head and take a few sips of water. "What did you have to tell her about my condition?"

Michelle tries to be casual, but the worry spills over in her voice. "Just that you're under a doctor's care and have been doing fine. But every once in a while, you get attacks like this where your blood pressure spikes, and it seems like you're having a heart attack, even though you're not." She leans my head towards her and kisses it, then caresses my cheek. "You gave me quite a scare back there, honey. We're all very concerned about your mother, and I know you're going to want to be there 24/7 for her, but you've got to promise me you'll take care of yourself too when we get back."

I look at my wife with grateful, sleepy eyes. "I promise, baby. I'll make an appointment with Doctor Jacobs soon." An involuntary yawn breaks through. "I better get some rest now before we land."

⟩ Chapter 7 ⟨

It is an unbearable sight, an immense weight burying all of us. Kennedy, Dad, Michelle, and I stare at Ma, horrified as she lays in the surgical ICU. An oxygen mask covers her battered and bandaged face. She is barely recognizable; large purple-red bruises and swelling consuming her face. Ma's head is shaved and wrapped in bandages to cover the area where a neurosurgeon drained blood from her brain.

"Have the doctors been by yet today?" I ask quietly.

"Around six a.m. They thought she was doing pretty well considering everything she's been through," Dad says in a whisper.

"Yeah, we're lucky she's still…" I rub my stubbled, worn face with my hand. All the stress, almost twenty-two hours of travel, and the extreme time change are catching up to me. "It's good to see her hanging in there so well," I say, feigning optimism.

Michelle lets go of my hand to wipe tears from the edges of her eyes. She sniffles and looks at each of us in turn. "Jackie's the strongest person I know. She'll pull through." The tears come freely now as her face collapses onto itself. "She's got to."

I rest my head on Michelle's and hug her. "She will, honey, she will."

"Oh gosh, I just need a few minutes," Michelle exclaims as she breaks away and looks at me tentatively. "Um, I'm gonna go check on the kids." I close the door behind Michelle as she slides out of the room and heads for the waiting area downstairs.

I glance at my father, seated, sheets strewn about the chair, pillow on the floor. He pulls out Ma's pink android phone and stares at the screen, his face filled with pain. "She was about to send me this text when she was attacked."

I take the phone from Dad and swallow hard as I read the message. "Hi, sweetie. Hope our lovely grandchildren aren't terrorizing you too much, lol! I got the strawberry oatmeal you asked for and the Italian candy the kids love so much. Tonight, I'll make your favorite dinner and brownies with the kids. Looking forward to your lovely hugs and kisses later." The message was followed by a smiley face emoticon and another one of a big kiss.

My heart sinks as I look Dad in the eyes and put a hand on his shoulder. I desperately wish for a way to ease his pain. "How are you holding up, Dad? It's been a helluva twenty-four hours."

"I'll say. But don't worry about me, Chris, I'm hanging in there." His quiet tone betrays the words he speaks. I hand him back the phone.

"Why don't you grab some food, Dad? You need your strength and there's nothing to do here right now. Kev and I will let you know if anything changes."

"Yeah, okay." He rubs the back of his neck and twists his head as he gets up from the chair. "Stretching my legs and clearing my head sounds like a good idea." He gives me a brief hug and then pats my face before heading towards the door. Halfway through, he turns back. "Let me know right away if anything changes."

"Will do, Dad."

Kennedy and I make eye contact. We can both speak freely now. My sorrow and anguish have coalesced over the last day into rage. "We have to nail the fucker who did this to Ma."

"My thoughts exactly, Chris," he says through gritted teeth.

"I know this is far from your precinct in Midtown Kev, and I don't want you sticking your neck out for Ma and me, but were you able to find anything out?"

Kennedy, my best friend and confidante these last twenty-three years, doesn't hesitate, "Chris, I'd go to war for you and your family, you know that. The shit situation I grew up in, with my old man beating my mother, sister, and me regularly.... My poor mom never had a chance, but that didn't stop your mom from doing her best to try and help her. Taking her to the doctors, to support groups, trying to get her the hell out of that situation. Shit, Sam and I practically lived with you guys when our father was going off the deep end." Kennedy's teeth are grinding hard now; his eyes shine like lasers. He looks like he can shred steel between his teeth. "Your mom was always there for me and my family. Whoever did this to her is gonna pay – big time."

"Chief of Detectives Ray Petersen understands the situation and he pulled some strings. I'm the invisible part of precinct 4-8's investigation, which is just the way I like it," Kennedy says with eyes ablaze. "We've got two eyewitnesses, one Fordham student taking some summer classes, and a woman, an employee on break from the botanical gardens."

"What'd they see?"

"Your typical low-life staged accident turned mugging. One guy was laying down next to a car with a bloodied shirt. The other guy waved down your mom and then jumped her when she came over to help."

"Shit, that scenario is perfect bait for someone like Ma. She'd stop and help Satan look for his pitchfork if she thought she could be helpful. Fuck!"

"Apparently, your mom put up a hell of a fight. Kicking and screaming, scratching one guy's face and eye up pretty bad and biting the other's forearm." Kennedy pauses as we both smile with pride. "Our perps must have planned to rob her, maybe steal her car, but she kept them so busy they were spooked and took off by foot down Southern Boulevard towards the Mosholu Parkway. They might have had some help getting away from there. The officers on the scene couldn't find them when they got there a few minutes later."

I ponder what Kennedy just said. "So you're practically invisible on this, huh?"

"Yup, just call me Casper – minus the friendly part," he growls.

Our eyes lock again. "You know what this means, right?" I say.

"Damn straight. Anybody misses anything on this investigation, I'll be all over it," Kennedy says with determination. "Nothing is gonna stop us from bringing your mother's attackers to justice."

I smile at Kennedy. "When retribution rains down on those two punks, they'll wish they mugged the devil himself instead."

▷ Chapter 8 ◁

The last five days since we rushed back home are a blur. I am exhausted through and through and an emotional wreck. Being up now at 4:30 a.m. isn't helping the situation.

"Are you sure you're going to be okay going back to work tomorrow, honey?" Michelle asks warily as she lightly rests her hand on my forearm. "No offense, but you don't look so good."

Worry lines cut deep canyons in my face as we sit in the kitchen in our pajamas and bathrobes, cold coffee mugs in front of us. My hair is a mess, and five days of jagged stubble dominate my face. "Thanks for the pick me up, babe. You look like a million bucks, too," I grumble as I pull my arm away.

Michelle deserves thanks, not sarcasm. As always, her sole concern is my well-being. Mom and she share an almost pathological need to make everyone else happy before they can feel the same way. So why the hell did I just say that?

Michelle sits upright, a pained look on her face.

I reach out to touch her hair, but she pulls back.

"I'm sorry for being such a jerk, baby. I don't know what the hell is wrong with me." I exhale hard, my breath infused with self-loathing and frustration. "I know this is as hard on you as it is on me."

Michelle breaks down, burying her face in her hands. Her words come in fits between the sobbing. "It is hard, Chris.... Your mom means the world to me.... Without her, I don't know how I would have survived my mom dying while we were at Fordham." The tears come full force now. What an idiot I was to snap at her! I put one arm over her shoulder and lean in so Michelle can rest her head on my chest.

"I know it's hard, baby, but we'll get through this, somehow," I say, hoping my lack of faith isn't obvious.

"Oh my God, it hurts so much." Michelle buries her head farther in my chest, her hot tears soaking my pajamas. Minutes drag by before Michelle speaks up. "Your mom is the best. When my mother died I was *so* depressed. I couldn't get out of bed in the morning, didn't want to go to classes or even eat anything." A pained smile fills Michelle's face. "Even though your mom and I didn't know each other that well then, she made it her mission to help me through my grief. I owe her my life, Chris."

I smile back at Michelle. "In one way or another, we all owe Ma our lives." Tears stream down my face now too.

Michelle kisses my tears and draws me into a hug. Our bodies share the stillness, the silence, and the sorrow. Michelle is the first to pull away.

"Whatever happens, honey, we need to be there for each other – unconditionally. No matter what it takes, what sacrifices we need to make, we have to pull each other through this. It's what your mom would want," she says with a sad smile.

Michelle's words help both of us regroup and gather strength.

"I'm worried about you, Chris. I know how much pressure you put on yourself all the time," she says, a pained smile breaking over her face.

I reach out and cup her hands in mine. "I'll be okay. Maybe work will help take my mind off things with Mom, make me feel better by helping others."

"Maybe...I just know your work is all-consuming, with no margin for mistakes." Michelle shifts her hands so ours are now interlaced. She clears her throat. Her tone is cautious, careful as the tears dry on her cheeks. "I know the last thing you want is to not be there for your patients, Chris. Going back so soon, though, might put you and them in a difficult situation. Are you sure you're ready?"

"I hope so. But to be honest, I have no idea." My

eyes are downcast and sullen. "It's been almost a week since Ma was attacked and she's still a mess, which means I'm still a mess."

"Maybe you can have someone cover for you? They must understand how hard this is for you."

"It would be tough last minute like this. A lot of attending physicians at teaching hospitals like ours take time off in July and August. No one wants to oversee the new residents' nightmarish performance on their first cases. That's part of the reason we took some time off too. I mean Peters is showing promise, but I've still got to be on top of his every move so he doesn't fu-, er, mess anything up. But, getting back to your point, there's just nobody around to cover for me. Besides, I don't want to start my work as an attending with such a show of weakness."

"Weakness? Your mother's in a coma after a brutal attack! No one can blame you for being upset about that," Michelle says with a shriek. "What do they expect, you to be a robot or something?!"

I run a hand through my hair, anxiety creeping into my voice. "I know what you're saying, Michelle, but surgeons are supposed to be superhuman. We can't let anything get to us. Hell, the job is hard enough already. If distractions start creeping in, patients start dying."

Michelle tilts her head to the side. "So...what are you going to do?"

I pull back, my palms facing upward as I shrug. "Guess I'm just going to give it all I got and hope for the best," I say weakly.

⊳ Chapter 9 ⊲

"**S**hould I make the incision here for the trocar, Doctor Ravello?"

"Huh, yeah, yes, that will be fine, Peters." My focus is shit right now. I love performing surgery, but I didn't think it would be so hard to jump back in. "We'll place the last one there and have this gall bladder out in no time," I say with feigned confidence and conviction. "First laparoscopic case, right Peters?"

The next few minutes glide by, my lapses not as long or as frequent. I seem to be winning the battle. I look up for a moment from the monitor that guides our progress, draw in a deep breath, and then refocus on the task at hand. "Shit, Peters, what are you doing?! No, no, don't cut that. That's the cystic artery, not the cystic duct. Oh God..." The field is all bright red with blood. "Quick, we've got to open him up!"

"Sssorry, Doctor Ravello. I must've nicked it."

Peters' voice and those of the nurse and anesthesiologist sound far off, unintelligible, as I race to open up our patient's right side.

Blood soaks through multiple 4 x 4 gauze pads as we suction and cauterize, desperate to gain control of the situation.

This case, which should have been a breeze for me, is an interminable nightmare. The patient, with a preexisting cardiac condition, is in crisis. Anticoagulants that thin his blood are causing him to bleed out. "Transfuse four units. Get four more ready. We need it NOW!"

For twenty minutes the OR staff and I battle one setback after another, but it is to no avail. Our patient's sick heart cannot handle the extensive blood loss. At 8:42 a.m. our anesthesiologist gently pulls me away from the body after declaring our patient dead.

I stare at the muted, lime-green OR walls in disbelief as the staff cleans up. The agony and grief I feel over Mom are now multiplied. This should never have happened. I let this case get away from us. My lapses in concentration have cost this man his life, just as surely as the injuries from Ma's mugging may yet take hers.

▷ Chapter 10 ◁

Kennedy and I sit quietly at a back table at the Rye Bar and Grill. I have just finished spilling my guts about the disastrous case I had earlier, admitting how difficult it is for me to focus on my work. I can't get my mind off Ma.

"I can't even imagine doing what you do, Chris, let alone doing it with such a heavy heart," Kev says, his voice tinged with sadness, empathy, and respect.

"Yeah, I don't know what the hell I'm going to do. There's no way to make this right, no way for me to bring him back. I can't keep putting patients at risk but I'm stuck. There's nobody around to cover for me." Needing some hope, some glimmer of light at the end of the tunnel, I change the subject. "So where exactly are we in Ma's investigation, Kev?"

"You want the good news first or the bad news?" Kennedy can see what a wreck I am. "Yeah, so let's go with the good news first," he says with a nod. He raises his beer to his lips and takes a sip while I fidget with my hands and the napkin in front of me.

"The Fordham student I told you about and the botanical garden's worker each got a clear view of both suspects. The student even recorded them on his phone as they fled the scene."

"That's great!" I exclaim.

"Yeah, definitely. After analyzing the cell phone footage and running the student and worker through the mug shot books, McGregor and Finelli, the local cops working the case, came up with positive IDs."

I hold my breath for a beat, then two, sensing what hangs in the air between us.

"But..." I say.

"After interviewing the suspects' known associates and then staking out their cribs for a few days, they came up with nothing, absolutely nothing."

"No sign of the losers? Shit! What the hell are their names? Have they got records?" I spit out.

Kennedy doesn't flinch at my ranting. "Teddy Gonzalez and Derrick Damples. They have a few minor priors: shoplifting, vandalism, and the like. Nothing to get too excited about."

My impatience spills over. "So, where does that put us now?"

"I don't know, Chris, but McGregor and Finelli's Chief then told them to put the case on the back burner. 'Concentrate on more pressing matters,' was how he put it."

"Are you fucking kidding me?!" I exclaim.

A middle-aged woman in a flowery dress seated at a nearby table looks at me, mortified and disgusted. She shakes her head in disapproval, then whispers something to her husband before she resumes eating.

"Wish I was, buddy. Wish I was."

I rub my face with both hands then blow out a sigh. "Well, that cinches it. We've got no choice. The Bash Brothers are back in business."

Growing up together as outcasts in Ossining, we got in a lot of trouble. We were always fighting the locals and skirting the law. We named ourselves after the Oakland A's sluggers of the late 80s and early 90s, Mark McGwire and Jose Canseco. During Kennedy's ten year stint with the NYPD and for me college, med school, and residency, we had resurrected the Bash Brothers here and there to right some wrongs. Those cases were intense, but nothing compared to this.

"Your neck is more on the line with this than mine, Kev, so how exactly do you want to handle this?"

"I've got it all worked out, my friend," Kennedy says with a broad smile that gives me the hope I so desperately need. "Here's how we'll play it...."

⊳ **Chapter 11** ⊲

Michelle tears up as we sit stiffly in our bed, her hand resting on my back. "I, I don't know what to say, Chris," she says in disbelief.

"Yeah," I reply with a shake of my head. "I've replayed it a million times in my head. How could I be so stupid? So careless?"

A pained look on her face, Michelle leans in and rests her hands and head on my shoulders. "You're doing the best you can," she says hollowly.

"That's not good enough," I choke out, riddled with guilt.

We sit alone in silence, my brain a jumbled mess. *Where do we go from here?* I wonder. Finally, I speak, peppering Michelle with questions to change the subject, the mood. "How are the kids? Any updates on Ma?"

"The kids are fine. They're so young they don't

really understand what's going on. Ma is about the same. Hasn't regained consciousness yet."

"I want to be there for all of them. Kills me I didn't see any of them tonight." Exhausted and upset, I slump forward.

"You did what you had to do tonight, honey. Any update from Kev?"

"Yeah, good and bad news. The officers working the case identified the muggers but were then told to focus on other, more pressing cases when they didn't make any progress locating them."

"So what happens now?" Michelle leans forward, clinging to me.

I stare ahead, not sure how to broach the subject. Michelle always supports me one hundred percent. The Bash Brothers? Not so much.

My voice is filled with hesitation. "I guess that leaves it up to Kennedy and me if we want to unofficially pursue things."

"If it was anybody other than your mom, Chris, I would say leave it to the police. Kennedy doesn't need to risk trouble at work, and with two young kids, a new job, and an expensive new house, neither do you. But it is Ma," Michelle says with determination, "and whoever did this has to be brought to justice. And I know helping with that will make it much easier for you to deal with what's happened to her. Just promise me you'll be careful, honey."

Relief washes over me as I wrap my arms around Michelle. "Thanks, baby. I will."

"How is your condition? Any attacks, since the plane ride, you haven't told me about?"

"The pheo? Uh, not really. I'm holding my own with it," I lie.

"Well, you better go see your doctor, like you promised, just to be sure."

"Who has time for that with everything else going–"

Michelle's stern gaze catches me like a shot to the head.

I backtrack. "Uh, absolutely. How can I take care of my family if I don't even take care of myself? I'll make an appointment in the morning."

Michelle smiles. "That's what I want to hear." She leans in for a kiss and rubs my head. "Now let's try and get some sleep."

▷ Chapter 12 ◁

My endocrinologist leans back from me, stethoscope held in one hand, a serious look on his face. "I'm worried about you, Chris. I'm also tired of reminding you to be careful." He shakes his head from side to side. "You know as well as I do, inoperable pheochromocytoma is not to be taken lightly."

I begin to protest, but a raised hand traps the words in my throat. "Yes, you've managed it well throughout the years, by keeping the stress in your life under control and staying physically fit. However,..."

"What...?"

He shakes his head in disgust, his patience wearing thin. "The flood of adrenaline you get with each attack has the potential to cause serious organ damage if left unchecked. So far you've been lucky that hasn't been the case. At some point, that luck will run out."

Jacobs' lecture is nothing new. I've heard it each

visit since he diagnosed me as a surgical intern. Every time, Jacobs advocates curtailing stress as much as possible. I promise to comply, knowing I will fail miserably.

"Then what?" I force a smile. "Remember, I'm just a lowly surgeon. We don't understand all this hormone stuff. We're just good with knives."

In all my years under Jacobs' care, humor has never worked on him. I don't know why I thought today would be any different.

"Repeated severe attacks can cause damage to your heart, kidneys, liver, or lungs. This damage can lead to death or disability." Jacobs' eyes narrow beneath his black rimmed glasses.

A glimmer of humanity breaks through the doctorly veil. "Talk to me, Chris. Your blood pressure is up now. You report a few attacks recently after not having one for almost two years. What's going on lately that's setting you off?"

"Well, let's see...I'm a newly ordained surgical attending, managing the latest crop of inexperienced residents at one of the busiest trauma centers in the country. Just took on a seven figure mortgage for a dream home on the Rye waterfront that Michelle fell in love with. Oh, and one other thing."

Jacobs' face is impassive. "Yes?"

"My mother was brutally beaten in front of the Bronx

Botanical Gardens. She had a large hematoma drained from her brain and has yet to regain consciousness."

"That's terrible, Chris. Your mother is the salt of the earth. Any idea who would want to do this to her?" Jacobs asks with concern.

"Funny you should ask. I've been helping Kennedy with an unofficial investigation, and we have a strong lead on the suspects."

Why the hell was I telling Jacobs this? He's my doctor, not my priest or confidante. Still, he's familiar with the cast of characters in my life, and I need someone outside of my family and Kennedy I can vent to.

"What?! You, a trauma surgeon, are assisting your NYPD detective friend in an unsanctioned investigation. Chris, have you lost your mind?"

Hmm, maybe Jacobs wasn't the best guy to share with right now.

"Uhh, does sound a bit crazy, huh? Kennedy's got unofficial approval for his part in the investigation and is working on getting the same for me." My voice trails off as I see Jacobs' slack-faced expression. "I'm guessing you're not enamored with my plan?"

Jacobs shakes his head, starts to speak, stops, and then starts again. "Does Michelle know about this?" Jacobs shakes his head, vigorously this time. "Why am I even asking this? I'm your endocrinologist, not your drinking buddy." Jacobs' exasperation is palpable. "Besides, I already know the answer. You downplayed the risks to Michelle and have left out some of the more worrisome details of your plan and your health of late. Am I right?"

A self-conscious smile spreads across my face. "Yup, that's about right." Jacobs knows me too well to bother with a denial.

He looks towards the ceiling and shakes his head yet again, then bores holes in my skull with his bespectacled gaze. "I hope you know what the hell you're doing, Chris. You've got a lot at stake here, and I'm not sure how much more of this your body can handle."

⟩ Chapter 13 ⟨

Outwardly Mom's improvement is dramatic. The bruises on her face are receding and the bandages on her skull have been removed. Hair is starting to grow over the large scar on her head. Yesterday they even transferred her out of the surgical ICU to the private room she is in now. But a face mask persists to keep her oxygen level up, and myriad tubes and monitors maintain their hold on her. I glance at Dad, who looks like he has aged five years in the last week and a half. The news from Ma's neurosurgeon continues to be worrisome.

"It's still early, Mr. Ravello. Anything could happen. But there is a chance your wife may not regain consciousness. The trauma to her brain was severe."

Dad reflexively hunches forward and steadies himself on the bed. As a homicide detective for two decades, he delivered more than his share of bad news to loved ones. Being on the receiving end of it, well, it's unfamiliar territory for him.

I lean forward to support him. "You okay, Dad?"

He shifts his body and stands tall, resolute. "I'm fine, Chris, thanks." He crosses his arms over his chest in a show of strength, composure.

"Doctor, we spoke just after you operated on my mother and then a few days later. I don't know if you remember me?"

"Yes, of course, Doctor Ravello. You're on the general surgery and trauma service over at Washington General, right?"

I nod affirmatively. "I realize Mom's situation doesn't seem promising, but..." I look over at Dad, then continue, "but we want to make sure we continue to do everything possible to pull Mom through this."

"Of course, Doctor Ravello, I understand. I'll keep you apprised of her condition." He looks at my father, then me. "The nurse's station has my office number. Don't hesitate to call. With my busy schedule, I realize I can be difficult to reach." The doctor gives a quick nod and begins to retreat towards the door.

"One last thing, Doctor. I noticed a small, diamond-shaped area of scarring on the right side of Mom's neck that I can't account for. It's as if she was punctured by something. See?" I say, pointing out the small mark on her skin.

The neurosurgeon peers at Mom's neck. "Hmm, very strange...I can't say I noticed that before."

We stare at each other for a moment, both perplexed. "Well, I don't want to hold you up anymore. Thank you, Doctor."

He nods, then backs through the door, just missing Kennedy.

"Excuse me, Doctor," Kev says. The neurosurgeon is shocked by Kennedy's height and girth.

"Quite all right. My fault," he stammers as he escapes.

Kennedy and I exchange a quick hug before he and Dad do the same.

"How's she doing?" Kennedy asks me with downcast eyes.

"Not much change I'm afraid."

We both look at Ma, then at Dad, who is seated on the side of the bed holding her hand. Tears form at the fringes of Dad's lower eyelids.

"You're the strongest woman I know, Jackie. Keep fighting. We're gonna find a way to pull you through this, honey, whatever it takes."

I choke back my anger and sorrow. Acknowledging Dad's need for some alone time with Ma, Kennedy and I slip into the hallway.

"We set for later?" I ask Kev.

"Yeah, just let me know what time you free up and we'll pay him a visit. Everything set on your end?"

"Yeah. I borrowed what I needed from work. We're good."

Kennedy studies my face. "You okay, buddy? You look confused or something," he says with concern.

"Yeah, I am. I just found a strange, diamond-shaped scar on Mom's neck. Neither her doctor nor I know what to make of it." I pause and shake my head slowly. "It might be nothing given all her other injuries...or it could be from her attackers. Maybe they injected her with something to make it easier to subdue her."

Kennedy rubs his chin as he mulls things over. "Mind if I take a look?"

We step into Mom's room, startling Dad. "Everything okay?" he says.

"Yeah, I just need to show Kev something."

Kennedy leans in and studies the scar carefully. "Yeah, that's the same one." He rises to his full height and then signals for me to join him back outside.

"What's up?" I say.

"One of the guys from my precinct was telling me about a weird case the other day, an attempted abduction of an elderly man in Queens that the local beat cops broke up. Turns out the vic had a scar just like your mom's." A determined look fills Kennedy's face. "We may have a serial offender here, and if you're right about the injections, Chris, there may be a medical angle to these crimes."

"Which would bolster my case for helping out with Ma's investigation," I say with a bright smile.

"Exactly."

Kennedy and I spend the next ten minutes squaring away details for later and discussing the meeting he has in a few hours with the New York City Mayor, the police commissioner, and the governor. If all goes according to plan, Kennedy will have permission for me to partake in the investigation before he and I pursue things on our own tonight. I thank him for everything before he leaves, then I return to Mom's room.

"Where'd Kev go? Everything all right?" Dad asks with concern. "How about that scar you were showing him on your mother?"

"He had some work stuff to take care of. Yeah, he's fine. As for the scar, it's small, but we're checking into it."

Dad peers at me, waiting, an old detective trick I'm sure. Finally, I relent, filling him in on my difficulties at work, my frustration with the investigation, and Kev's and my plans to unofficially help track down the muggers.

"Son, no one knows better than me the vagaries of detective work. We all want to catch who did this to your mother, but you should leave the investigating to the police. Our main concern now is doing everything we can to help your mother heal."

"I know, Dad, but I've got to do something, anything, to help," I implore. An unformed thought nags at me as it tries to take shape.

"You're doing plenty already. You're spending a ton of time around here, and you've got to be around for Christine and James too. Not to mention your work and paying the bills on that beautiful new home of yours." Dad smiles for the first time since Ma's attack. "You're doing a great job juggling things without adding detective work to your list of responsibilities." He pauses, his voice filled with concern. "How's Michelle holding up? She and your mom are so close. This has got to be hard on her too."

"She's hanging in there, Dad." I consider my next words carefully. "She's onboard with my moonlighting duties," I say firmly.

"What?!" Dad grumbles a few things under his breath, before putting the matter behind us.

Neither one of us wants or needs a confrontation now. We'll just have to agree to disagree – not easy for two stubborn, hot-blooded, Bronx-bred Italians.

I stare down at the floor for a minute, trying unsuccessfully to piece together the thought that eludes me. Stress and exhaustion are taking their toll on me, and yet I have to be back at work in less than two hours. My thoughts are jumbled, disconnected. I look back at Dad. He speaks first. "Chris, this sitting around here helpless is killing me. I wish there was something more we could do to help your mother." A strange look crosses Dad's face as he stares at the door, pondering the situation, then continues, "I wish, somehow, some way, Emily could walk through that door right now and be with us. Losing your sister all those years ago, I thought it would kill your mother and me. I can't go through that same pain again with your mother."

Dad scans the instruments, tubes, and IV's that surround Mom before he says, half serious, "Any miracle cures we haven't considered?"

I rock back and forth, teeth clenched, realizing my brain is searching for the same thing – a cure for Ma. "There may be something...it's unorthodox, for sure, and I don't want to step on any of Ma's doctor's toes, but hell, we just can't keep twiddling our thumbs. I'm going out to the nurse's station to look through Ma's chart if they'll let me. I've been so wrapped up in my grief, I just assumed the doctors here are doing everything they can for Ma," I say, exasperated with my inadequacies. "But, maybe they're missing something."

I catch a glimmer of hope in Dad's eyes, the same glimmer he, no doubt, now sees in mine. I hope we're not deluding ourselves. "That's a great idea, Son," he says excitedly. "You're a surgeon, you may be able to suggest something her doctors didn't think of."

I nod slowly. 'No telling how long this will take. Kennedy and I have something set up for later, but I'll postpone that. Ma's life may depend on what I come up with."

▷ **Chapter 14** ◁

Detective First Grade Kevin Kennedy sits on one side of the conference table at One Police Plaza. Governor Gregory Spatick, New York City Police Commissioner John Kelly, and New York City Mayor Michael Blumenthal form a firing squad across from him. At least that's how it feels to Kennedy.

"So, Detective Kennedy, what is so important that you need the police commissioner, our dear mayor, and myself all present?" Sarcasm fills the expanse between Kennedy and the pompous, self-indulgent prick, Spatick. "We're waiting," he says with annoyance.

Kennedy stares at Spatick, sizing him up. He'd love to give the loathsome governor a good throttling. Back in April, he denied critical state funding for the NYPD's counter-terrorism bureau until the mayor kowtowed to his political demands. *Everyone in this room hates the guy, yet he always comes out on top. So, instead of beating the crap out of this weasel, I'll use his power to my advantage.*

"As you know, Governor, Congress recently provided funding for states to establish a Division of Medical Crimes. The DMC investigates any and all crimes felt to be medical or scientific in nature, such as those involving doctors, hospitals, pharmaceutical companies, medical or scientific groups–"

"Yes, yes, I know, Detective," Spatick says impatiently. "I don't need a history lesson. I established the New York State DMC months ago and by Congressional mandate, I am in charge of it, so I know the facts better than anyone." Spatick's pedantic and condescending tone continues, annoyance carved across his face. The three of us are well aware of these facts, Detective, so what is your point?"

Blumenthal and Kelly look at Spatick. The former masks his disapproval well. The latter clenches his hands, anxious to introduce Spatick to the sharp edges of his fists.

Kennedy fights to maintain his composure. *Spatick is an even bigger asshole than I remember him being,* he thinks. But, losing his cool is not an option for Kennedy right now. Chris badly needs his help. And by Kennedy's analysis, the DMC needs his friend just as much. So Kennedy replies, coolly, "It's just as you said, governor. You are in charge of the DMC – for now anyway."

Spatick's face contorts in anger. "What the hell are you talking about, Detective?" Spatick says with intensity.

Kennedy keeps his cool. "The money the Feds provided to establish the DMC came with conditions. Buried deep in all the Washington legalese is an explanation of those conditions." Kennedy pulls the papers out of his jacket pocket and slides them across the table to Spatick. "I circled the relevant passages, governor."

Blumenthal leans towards Spatick, the two reading the passages together. Kelly sits upright, his face devoid of expression as he waits for his detective to continue.

Spatick speaks first. "This says the Feds can take over or disband any state DMC that has been in existence for at least one year if it is found to be ineffective. Once again, so what?"

Kennedy eyes Kelly with caution. This next part will be awkward, no question about it. He shifts his gaze to Spatick. "Our DMC is based in New York City and works as an independent division of NYPD. Commissioner Kelly's office confirmed my suspicions. Nearly three months and thirty-four investigations into their existence, the DMC has yet to solve any cases. They haven't even made a single arrest."

Spatick glowers at Kelly. "Is that true, John?" Kelly shoots Kennedy a stern look before re-engaging Spatick. "'Fraid so, governor. Nobody in the DMC has any medical training whatsoever. We're a bit out of our element with these cases. But that will change as we gain experience. Give us a little more time and–"

"Are you kidding me, John? Three months is an eternity in New York politics and the Feds can take over soon if we don't make some arrests. I stuck my neck out when I became the first governor to establish a DMC." He looks at Kennedy, Kelly, and Blumenthal in rapid succession. "I have no intention of having it chopped off because of investigative ineptitude." Spatick's attention returns to Kennedy, his eyes ablaze. "So, Detective, I assume you're bringing this up because you have a proposal to rescue the DMC from itself?"

Kennedy looks over at Kelly, who is fuming. The detective gave him a heads-up earlier about wanting to bring Chris onto this investigation but didn't mention anything about Chris running the DMC going forward. Kennedy sizes up the situation. *Moment of truth, so here goes.* "I know a physician who might be interested in heading up the DMC."

Surprise and skepticism flood Spatick's face, but he keeps uncharacteristically silent as he calculates all the angles before proceeding. "Interesting proposal, Detective Kennedy. The DMC can certainly use new, medically trained leadership. But what does a physician know about police work, and why in God's name would one want to trade his stethoscope for a gun?" He pauses. "And how do we even know this physician can handle detective work?"

So far so good. He replies casually, "This one; it's in his blood. His father served as an NYPD detective for over twenty years."

Intrigued, Spatick probes further, speaking to no one in particular. "Who is this father and son?"

Kelly sees an opening, a chance to seize control. He interjects. "Bill Ravello is the father. He worked out of the 48th precinct. A great cop and even better man. His son, Doctor Chris Ravello, is a trauma surgeon over in Harlem at Washington General. He's got no investigative experience whatsoever."

Spatick nods slowly, taking it all in. "Good lineage... and the press will eat up the father-son connection. But why would the son want to help us? What's in it for him, Detective?"

Kelly's jaw clenches tight as Spatick again by-passes him.

This next part will be the trickiest to steer through, Kennedy thinks. *I'll have to be careful how I present Chris' motives. Vengeance and vigilantism would be poorly received.* Kennedy leans onto his right forearm, then shifts so he sits upright. He towers over Spatick and the others. "He's recently suffered a personal tragedy. His mother was brutally attacked by muggers in front of the Bronx Botanical Gardens. She's in a coma now at Jacobi Medical Center. Doctor Ravello has expressed a desire to assist me – unofficially, of course – in apprehending the men who attacked his mother." Kennedy scans their faces. "Earlier today, we found the same medical connection to two cases, Mrs. Ravello's attack and that of a recent assault in Queens. These medically based crimes give the NYPD an excellent opportunity to evaluate Doctor Ravello's performance under the most difficult of circumstances. The benefits for Doctor Ravello are two-fold. He gets peace of mind from helping to put away his mother's attackers. He also gets a preview of life as a detective. If he enjoys it, the DMC is a natural segue for him into police work if he so chooses."

"That's all well and good, Detective," Kelly responds. "But working one case to put away his mother's attackers is a far cry from leaving behind a career in medicine to pursue detective work full time. I don't see how this helps with our DMC problem."

"Not so fast, John. I like what I'm hearing so far. Continue, Detective," Spatick says smugly.

"Doctor Ravello is very much an idealist. The idea of helping other families avoid the heartache his family has been through will be very appealing to him. The DMC would allow him to pursue justice while continuing to make use of his medical and scientific training."

"This will likely be a waste of time, governor," Kelly chimes in. "In the end, there are no assurances

Doctor Ravello will choose the DMC over his medical career."

"He's the perfect fit, the perfect solution to your problem, governor," Kennedy responds.

Kelly looks ready to explode. He starts to lash out, but Spatick puts up his hand as a stop sign and smiles.

"Agreed, Detective. A noble, idealistic young surgeon leaves medicine behind to pursue police work after his mother is the victim of a violent crime. Very nice." He looks around the room. "We can all enjoy the PR boost this appointment will provide."

Blumenthal, a tall slender man with a well-earned reputation for impartiality, chimes in. "Governor, we share your enthusiasm for Doctor Ravello, but there are some other concerns as well."

Off balance, Spatick shoots back, "Such as?"

"For one thing, Doctor Ravello has no police training whatsoever. It would take him years to acquire the knowledge and skills necessary to run one of the busiest investigative units in the city," Kelly offers. "And we don't even know if he has the temperament and stomach for the work."

"Really, John? The doctor is a trauma surgeon in Harlem, for God's sake! He sees more blood and guts in one week than your boys see in a career," Spatick says with a wave of his hand. "As for the training...you know him well, Detective Kennedy?"

"Yes, sir. We grew up together." Kennedy glances

over at Kelly. *The commissioner will have my head if this scheme of mine fails.* "He's a quick study, governor, always has been."

"Good, good. We'll give Ravello the chance he's asking for. If he performs well and wants to move ahead, we'll send him through the police academy. When he graduates, we'll make him a detective third grade. He'll take over the DMC and work with Detective Kennedy, who will teach him the ropes of detective work."

Kelly is aghast. "Governor, it takes years on the street to become a detective, let alone a division chief. Ravello won't be prepared, and his men will resent the hell out of him for bypassing the normal channels. Surely–"

"How many years have you been on the NYPD, Detective Kennedy?" Spatick asks, ignoring Kelly again.

Oh great. Pit me against my boss even more. Kelly's gonna crucify me.

"About ten years, sir," Kennedy offers. "The last three as a detective first grade." Smoke pours out of Kelly's ears as his cheeks redden. He tries to interject, "Sir, I really think we need more time to consider–"

"All right, then, it's decided. Commissioner Kelly, Mayor Blumenthal, you're free to go. Detective Kennedy and I have some details to discuss." Spatick turns his back on the two men and continues with Kennedy. "Get Ravello in here ASAP so we can work out the details...."

▷ Chapter 15 ◁

Wedged into a small space between the nurses charting and break areas, I pour over Ma's chart. I begin with the ambulance call sheet, then review her hospital admission paperwork and progress notes from the nurses and physicians caring for her. Vitals, charting of Mom's fluid intake and output, and a copy of her operative report and CT and MRI scans of the head come next. It takes a little over forty minutes to go through it all, at which point I sign a medical records release form and the floor clerk is gracious enough to give me the two copies of Ma's chart that I need. I then head over to Washington General to touch base with two colleagues of mine, a neurosurgeon, Doctor Carl James, and a neurologist, Doctor Xin Hsu.

James, Hsu, and I have worked innumerable cases over the years, a handful eerily similar to Ma's. James is a skilled surgeon and clinician, and participates in a number of clinical trials. Perhaps he can offer Ma an intervention Jacobi's doctors can't.

Hsu is an astute diagnostician and researcher. As a neurologist, his thinking is decidedly conservative and non-surgical, which is exactly why I chose him. As a trauma surgeon, I naturally have a surgical bias, as does James. Hsu's opinion adds the necessary ballast about how to best treat Ma.

My first stop is James' office, an expansive space located on the third floor of Washington General's Medical Arts tower. A squat man with wavy salt and pepper hair and ever-present bags beneath his eyes, James listens intently to the details of Ma's case. "... and she's been unconscious at Jacobi ever since." I take a slow, deep breath as I sit across from him. "Any thoughts, Carl?"

"Hmm. A couple. Do you have a copy of the chart for me to review?" he says in a neutral tone.

I pull a copy out of my briefcase and slide it across the desk to him.

"Thanks. I'll take a look at it and call you later."

"That's all I can ask." I rise and shake his hand, "I'll look forward to your call."

Hsu is a tall, slender, impeccably dressed man in his mid-forties. Erudite and refined, Hsu and James could not be more dissimilar. Despite their differences, both are longstanding fixtures at Washington General, their offices just down the hall from each other. James and Hsu consult constantly on a wide array of cases throughout the hospital.

I extend my hand and a smile to him. "Hi, Xin. Thanks for agreeing to meet me so early."

He nods once. "But of course, Chris. It is my pleasure." He waves a hand towards his desk and chairs. "Please, have a seat, and tell me all about your mother's condition."

I fill Hsu in on all the particulars and provide him a copy of Ma's record. "You've consulted with Doctor James as well, I assume?"

Hsu and James often consult on the same cases, and if there is any discomfort in the arrangement, neither shows it. "Yes, of course, Xin."

Hsu pats the chart. "I will look through this carefully and discuss my opinion with Doctor James before reaching out to you later this morning."

I involuntarily nod, then stand up to shake his hand. "Great. I'm anxious to hear your thoughts. I'll let myself out."

§

In between a hernia repair and my first laparoscopic gall bladder removal since the death of my patient a few days earlier, I stop by the hospital's medical library. There I search Pub Med and other online repositories for any breakthroughs to help Ma. The main issue for her is the severe intracranial bleed she suffered and the swelling and contusions of her brain. These injuries were so acute and severe they have impaired her medulla, the part of the brain responsible for regulating breathing and heart function. Ma's doctors at Jacobi are implementing all the tried and true treatments for her, including various medications such as mannitol, intravenous steroids, and Lasix to improve her condition. They also surgically drained the blood and fluid collected on her brain. Unfortunately, none of these treatments brought Ma back to us.

Research confirms my own experience and my worst fears; if Ma doesn't wake up within the next few days, she likely never will.

The problem with my medical literature search is it does not turn up any drugs currently in clinical trials or that are just approved for treatment of cerebral swelling. Indeed, most of the articles I am finding just rehash the same treatment options and protocols.

The hope I felt earlier with Dad is dwindling away.

I am just about ready to give up and head back to the OR for my next case, when a call comes through from James.

"That was fast, Carl. Any good news?"

"Possibly," James responds. Caution fills his voice. "I have Xin Hsu with me here as well." Xin and I exchange pleasantries before James continues. "I'll need to examine your mother myself to be sure, but there is an investigative drug that may help her."

"That's fantastic! How quickly can she begin treatment if she qualifies?"

"Immediately," he responds before Hsu chimes in. "I must caution you, Chris, your mother's condition is grave, and there is scant data on the drug Doctor James refers to." I shift in my chair, ill at ease with the divergent opinions I elicited. Hsu continues, "Chris, it's as likely to kill your mother as it is to save her."

I draw in a tense breath. James and Hsu debate each other on the issue at hand as I tap my fingers on the workstation in front of me. My voice pierces theirs. "And if we continue on with her current treatment instead?"

Hsu answers. "We agree on this: without additional treatment, she may never regain consciousness. We have a day or two at most to act. After that, if she hasn't recovered, your mother may enter a permanently vegetative state or die outright."

I slump down in my chair, stunned at our limited options. "And we have no other treatment options either of you is aware of?" I imagine them looking at each other and shaking their heads in resignation.

"No, we don't," they respond in unison.

A tightness begins in my abdomen, then overtakes my chest. My gut tells me the drug is Ma's best bet, but the decision is agonizing. Do I continue on the current path and hope for a spontaneous recovery or intervene with a treatment that has as much a chance of killing her as curing her?

"Are you still there, Chris?" James asks.

"Yes, yes, I'm here," I gasp. "Just torn on what to do." I stare at the computer screen in front of me, knowing the answer isn't there. I hate to put my colleagues in this situation, but I do it nonetheless. "If she were your mother, what would you do?" Silence pervades the airwaves between us, the seconds dragging by.

"I'd give her the drug, Chris," James says. Hsu remains silent.

"Okay, well, there we have it. I've got to run this by my father to see which way we'll go. Thank you, Carl, Xin. I know this puts you both in a difficult position, and I appreciate your help. I'll get back to you later today."

§

I spend the next three hours struggling through two surgeries I should have breezed through in half the time. My brain is awash in thoughts of Mom and my conversations with Hsu and James. In between the surgeries, I resist the urge to squeeze in my phone call to Dad. As much as I want to get back to him and reach a conclusion, I realize this is a conversation best had in person.

Around 3:30 I climb into my 1974 Firebird and weave through Harlem and Bronx traffic until I arrive at Jacobi, confident I will find Dad perched at Ma's bedside. Listening to classical music on the drive over helped me clear my head and reset my outlook.

"Hey, Dad, any change?" I say brightly as I stride into Mom's hospital room.

"'Fraid not, Son, she's still totally out of it," Dad says with a grim expression. "How'd you make out looking through her chart and speaking with the other doctors?"

I stand frozen, unsure where to begin.

"You okay, Chris?" Dad says with concern.

"Yeah, I'm fine. Today's just been a blur, that's all. Not sure where to start."

"I understand. Take a minute and then just start wherever. We'll sort it out together," Dad replies.

I smile, appreciating Dad's homespun wisdom. I feel a weight lift off my shoulders.

"So, I didn't come up with much on the chart review, but I did get a neurosurgeon and a neurologist at Washington General to weigh in on what to do for Mom."

"And?" Dad replies cautiously.

"The neurosurgeon is involved in a clinical trial for a drug that *may* help Ma's condition. There's a chance it could help her to regain consciousness." Dad's face brightens. "It also could kill her."

"Shit. I thought..." Dad looks distant, lost. "What's the neurologist think?"

I come over and wrap my arm around Dad and give him a brief hug before continuing, "That's where things get really hairy. The neurologist thinks there is very little data on the new drug, so he cautions against using it. But, and this is the hard part, both doctors agree on one thing."

"What's that?"

"We've got to decide very soon what to do with Mom. Another day or two..." Tears fill my eyes as I turn my head away from Dad and try not to lose it, "and Mom might be beyond saving."

Dad pulls me towards him, his hand cradling the back of my head as he too fights back tears. We linger, time standing still.

Dad lets go of me and speaks. "Chris, your mother isn't getting any better on her own. If this drug is her only chance, we should take it."

"What if it kills her?" I protest.

Dad's face becomes solemn, the color draining from it. He looks over at Ma, pain taking him over. "Son, I think she's as good as dead like this." He wipes his eyes with the back of his sleeve, then places his hand on my shoulder. "You're the best son a mother or father could ever ask for. We're both so proud of the man you've become." Tears flow freely for both of us. "I know you're a doctor and want to do what's best for

Mom, but promise me this: we'll decide this together, okay? You can't add to your burden by putting this all on yourself. It's not fair, and your mother wouldn't want that." Dad pauses, his eyes connecting with mine. "Whatever we decide, whatever happens to Ma, we need to live with it and not beat ourselves up over our decision."

I nod in agreement, determined to make Dad feel better. But in my heart I know it is a false promise. If Ma dies, I won't be able to move on with the life I planned for myself. Dedicating my life and my life's work to her memory will be my only recourse, my only hope. What that means exactly, I do not know, but with body, brain, and spirit torn apart with grief, I know it just the same.

▸ Chapter 16 ◂

The decision to transfer Ma to Washington General firmly behind us, I set out with making the arrangements. I reach Mom's current neurosurgeon, via his answering service, and tell him of our decision. In Mom's current condition he feels transferring her to another facility is risky. "It could kill her" are his exact words. My reply summarizes the damned if you do, damned if you don't conundrum Dad and I find ourselves in. "She's basically dead already; we've got to try." And so we move forward.

In Mom's room, we make final preparations. "Dad, have you got all of Ma's belongings? The ambulance will be here any minute."

Dad looks around the room, happy to be bidding it goodbye, I'm sure, but wishing Ma's departure was under better circumstances. "Yeah, we're good. You riding over with her?"

"Yeah, I'd feel better that way. The EMT's won't be thrilled, but as a physician and her son, I refuse to honor any objections they may have," I say firmly.

Dad nods. "I'll head out now and drive your car over. A friend dropped me off yesterday, so we don't have to worry about my car."

Each of us leans over and kisses Ma on the forehead.

Three nurses appear at the door. "Doctor, Mr. Ravello. The ambulance is here," one of them says. "They're ready to take Mrs. Ravello." Dad gives me a quick hug and heads out as I look back at the nurses.

"I'll follow you all down. I'm going to ride over with her."

The nurses exchange uncomfortable glances, then busy themselves with the business of preparing Ma for transfer. The EMTs from the ambulance wait just outside her room.

Ma requires high levels of oxygen, IV fluids, and monitoring. We move her out of her room and make haste to get her into the ambulance. Any delays on the way to Washington General could prove fatal.

§

I am like a caged animal in the back of the

ambulance. It's well past the evening rush hour, yet traffic shows no signs of letting up on Pelham Parkway. Mom's breathing is already labored, her chest lurching forward with each inhalation. Two EMTs ride in the back with me instead of the normal one. It is an unspoken concession to how risky this ride is for Ma. Our lights flash and our siren wails, but they make little difference. Bronx drivers are long since habitualized to such spectacles.

"What the hell. Do we need to fire off some shots to get these cars moving?" I say to no one in particular. The EMTs make furtive eye contact, relieved I don't have a permit to carry. After an eternity, we finally make a right turn onto the Bruckner. With any luck, we are only twenty minutes away from Washington General. Traffic opens up for us as we chug Southbound on the expressway.

Mom's skin color begins to take on an ashen hue. Sweat beads on her face. The EMTs scramble to adjust her flow of oxygen and the pulse oximeter attached to her forefinger which measures her oxygen levels. The device shows her oxygen saturation drifting dangerously low.

"Shit! How much longer till we're there? She's gonna code at this rate," I yell.

And code she does.

The EKG reading goes flat-line. Mom's oxygen saturation plummets.

One EMT grabs adrenaline and pushes it in Ma's IV while the other begins chest compressions.

"Where's the intubation tray?" I yell. The first EMT throws a hermetically sealed pouch my way. In no time at all I have Ma's jaws open, her tongue clear, and the tube down her throat. I hook up the oxygen directly to her tubing and signal the second EMT to halt compressions as I check for breath sounds. I nod to him quickly. He resumes compressions in earnest.

The first EMT yells, "Paddles are charged. Clear." We jump back, staggering for firm footing as the ambulance careens through traffic. Electricity jolts Mom's body upward. "No good. Charging, 200 joules again. Resume compressions while we wait."

Ma's pulse ox dances into the low nineties, the highest reading since her heart stopped. Sweat drips off my forehead. My heart pounds against my chest. "All clear." The second electrical pulse ripples through Ma. Her EKG flutters, then catches. A normal sinus rhythm! She is going to make it!

"Pulling into Washington General now, Doctor Ravello," the driver yells frantically. "We should have your mom upstairs in no time."

§

Hsu and James bookend the entrance to Mom's private room.

"She okay, Chris?" James says as I emerge from her room, drained. "Holy shit! What a ride over here." Hsu stands stone-faced and silent, then ducks in the room to assess Mom.

"At least she's here now," James replies with relief. "I'm going to check on her now as well."

I pace the hall, then slow to a stop as I catch sight of Dad running towards me from the waiting area. I called him minutes earlier to fill him in.

Flustered, Dad blurts out, "How is she? Is everything all right?"

"Yeah, she's fine Dad." I grab his upper arms to calm him. "The neurologist and neurosurgeon are taking a look at her."

Hsu and James emerge from Mom's room, their faces indecipherable. I search their eyes for any clues.

"So?" I say.

James nods in deference to Hsu. "Your mother is recovering. We need to stabilize her for twenty-four to forty-eight hours before we attempt treatment."

"Isn't that cutting it close? You both thought we needed to treat her soon to make any difference," I point out.

They exchange a knowing glance. James speaks. "We don't have any choice, Chris. We've got to have her in better shape than this. In the best of circumstances, the medication stresses the body tremendously. We need her stronger." James looks at Dad and me in turn.

"You and your father should go home and rest. We'll touch base with you tomorrow when we know more."

I nod assent, then thank them both for everything. "Tomorrow it is." Dad and I turn and shuffle towards the elevator.

⟩ Chapter 17 ⟨

An involuntary laugh escapes my lips as I watch Christine demonstrate proper table manners to her brother.

"Now, James. You must keep your elbows off the table and don't eat your food with your fingers," Christine says with authority. "Mommy and Daddy said it's..." Christine looks over at Michelle and I, "Whatcha say, Mommy, bar-bari-un if we do it?"

Michelle lets cut a giggle as well. "That's right, honey. And barbarians are people with very poor table manners–"

"Who also smell really bad because they don't take baths regularly," I interject with a bright smile. "And we don't want to smell bad, right, kiddo?"

James looks on, bewildered, as his sister replies with her best stab at indignation. "Oh no, Daddy. Nobody wants to smell bad."

I look over lovingly at the mother of my children. Moments like these have been hard to come by since Ma was attacked. But, with everything we have been through and *will* be going through, we need these moments to keep us sane and anchored to what is important in life – love and family.

The doorbell rings. "I'll get it, honey," I say to Michelle as I rise and make my way to the front door. "May be Kennedy."

Sure enough, it is. "How we doing, buddy? Come on in."

Michelle wanders in from the kitchen, James at her hip, Christine holding her hand next to her. "Good to see you, Kevin. How's your day going?"

"Great, Michelle." Kennedy leans in and kisses her, then pulls out a few Hershey's kisses for the kids that have melted on the ride over. "How about some treats for Uncle Kevin's favorite niece and nephew?"

"Thank you," they sing in unison.

"We were just finishing up dinner. Can I get you something, Kev?" Michelle inquires.

"Sure, that'd be great. I'll meet you in the kitchen." With a nod to the right, towards my study, Kevin says, "Can I speak to you a second, Chris?"

A few moments later Kennedy and I settle into leather seats across from each other.

"Is this about the meeting with Spatick, Kev?"

Yeah. But first, how's your mom doing?"

I fill him in on yesterday's events, about how we almost lost her and the phone call from Hsu two hours earlier. "For now they have her stabilized." I bite my lower lip. "They'll give her the treatment in the morning."

"Thank God. She's strong, Chris. She's gonna pull through."

I wish for the same optimism. "I hope so, Kev." Images of Mom laying in that hospital bed, time running out, race through my mind. I shake my head, trying to clear it, as I struggle to focus on the here and now. "So, what happened with the meeting?" I say with little enthusiasm.

"Oh yeah. Well, Kelly and Blumenthal were there too, though you'd hardly know it. Spatick pretty much ignored them while he kept me on the hot seat."

I wait a few beats for my friend to continue while I ponder the situation. A couple of days ago, after my carelessness cost a patient his life, Kennedy and I agreed he would meet with the powers that be, seeking permission for me to help with the investigation into Ma's attack. It was a crazy request they'd dismiss outright – until Kennedy came up with a plan. He'd dangle my medical expertise before them, offering to help them solve a leadership issue they had at their newly formed Division of Medical Crimes, in exchange for my involvement in Ma's case. The strange scar we found on Mom's neck and that of another victim just bolstered our cause.

I badly wanted in on Ma's investigation, wanted to nail the bastards who attacked her. Kennedy and I had planned to track down a punk last night who knew Mom's attackers and pump him for information. But bringing James and Hsu into the mix, and all that followed yesterday, had reordered my priorities: get Mom better first, then nail her attackers. There was no time now for me to do both.

"Spatick is all over our idea, Chris. Blumenthal is more neutral on it, and Kelly, well, I think Kelly wants to tear off my head and shove it up my ass."

"That bad with Kelly, huh? We figured he'd be the tough one to sell on the idea," I say thoughtfully. "If Spatick backs me, he'll have no choice, since the governor has control over the mayor due to state budgeting issues that affect the city, and the mayor has control over the police commissioner. But things would work a lot better for both you and me if we can bring Kelly around."

"I agree. He's not going to listen to me now; he's too pissed. But, you're going to get your chance to explain yourself. I'm supposed to set up a meeting with the four of you to discuss things further. The sooner the better, according to Spatick."

"That's great, Kev. Looking forward to it."

"You don't sound too convincing, bud," Kennedy

replies. "You cool with this?" he says as he angles his monstrous neck while maintaining steady eye contact with me.

"I think so. It's just...the last twenty-four hours have been a whirlwind, and Mom's treatment is in the morning. She was supposed to have it today, but was in such bad shape last night they put it off." I wring my hands and shift uneasily in the chair. "I've been trying to put on a brave face for the kids and Michelle, but I'm really worried about the delay. Every hour that goes by without the medicine, Ma's chances of survival go down."

Kennedy's eyes search mine. "Hey, I get it. Things are crazy right now, and this is moving real fast. We can put off our investigating and the follow-up meeting a few days. They understand the situation."

Relieved I didn't have to be the one to say it, I continue, "Thanks so much for sticking your neck out for me, Kev. I really appreciate it, no matter what happens."

"Sure, don't sweat it. You'd do the same for me, I'm sure."

"Guys, come to the kitchen. I've got drinks and some food all ready for Kev," Michelle yells from down the hall.

"Be right there," I yell back before turning to my friend. "A couple of weeks ago life was great, and the sky was the limit for Michelle, the kids, and me. We moved into this fantastic house; I started earning some serious money as an attending; we were on an amazing vacation to Australia. Man, that all changed in a heartbeat." I look around. "Now, we're telling the most powerful men in the state a tale so I can help nail Ma's attackers, while she lays comatose, awaiting a life-saving medication," I say solemnly.

Kennedy smacks my shoulder with his hand. "Keep your chin up, Chris. Life can turn around just as quickly as it craps out. And hell, don't worry about those fuckers. Making them wait is no sweat, and you can bow out of the DMC gig once the investigation is over," he says with a laugh. "Now let's see what Michelle whipped up. I'm starving."

⟩ Chapter 18 ⟨

Dad, Michelle, and I huddle around the foot of Ma's bed. James and Hsu are off to our right, finishing up their examination of her.

"It's a go, Chris," James says with conviction.

I look at him, then Hsu, who adds, "I agree. We should begin now."

"What's the timeline on the treatment versus when we can expect to see results? Ten minutes? An hour?" I say in earnest.

"The drug has a unique chemical structure that allows it to penetrate the blood-brain barrier, but it takes time," Hsu replies. "We won't know anything for a few hours at least."

"And what about side effects? What are we looking for, and is it the same timeline?"

James handles this one. "The drug works by decreasing cerebral swelling and ramping up the brain's electrical activity. It basically shocks the patient into a conscious state."

Dad chimes in. "So, it's like a defibrillator for the brain, is that about right?"

"Exactly, Mr. Ravello. Except, unlike the defibrillator's momentary effect, the drug keeps the brain hyper-excited for anywhere from ten minutes to four hours, depending on the patient. The effect is remarkable. Patients awake quite lucid, as if they had never been injured." James looks at each of us in turn. "But the drug is unpredictable, its effects vanishing in an instant in some patients. You see, either the patient's brain heals and they return to normal for good..."

"Or they expire," I say, fear dripping from my lips.

Hsu cuts in. "Yes, that's correct, Chris."

"All right. We understand the risks. Are we all still in agreement?" I look around the room as everyone nods. "Good. Dad, Michelle, grab my hands. Doctors, I'd like to lead a short prayer." They bow their heads as we close our eyes.

"Lord, we ask you to provide our dear Jacqueline, light of all our lives, with your fortitude, your blessing, and your good fortune. We thank you for giving us these wonderful doctors to care for her and trust you will carry her through this treatment and back to us. Amen."

Dad, Michelle, and I share hopeful, cautious smiles. Michelle speaks through tear-draped lids, "That was beautiful, Chris."

Hsu steadies the ten-milliliter syringe and pierces the IV tubing with its needle. James adjusts the IV's rate of flow to match Hsu's delivery of the medication.

The miracle drug creeps into Mom's left antecubital vein, mixes with her blood, and begins its ascension to her brain.

We wait, silent and scared.

Ten minutes after administering the drug to Ma, Hsu, and James usher me away to care for my own patients, assuring me it will take hours to see an effect. Dad and Michelle stand vigil, promising to call as soon as anything changes.

§

Peters, the rest of the team, and I rush gunshot and stabbing victims up to the OR at breakneck speed. We see surgical consults for acute abdominal pain, unexplained gastric bleeds, and the like.

The hours drift by with no change in Mom's condition.

We round on our patients in the hospital and admit and discharge others – all before noon. Another typical day at Washington General. Except for how I feel about it. Detached. Disconnected. My mind on the patient who matters to me most.

On the bright side, I haven't killed anyone today – not yet anyway.

I sit in the corner of the dimly lit, dreary cafeteria picking at the remnants of my lunch: pulled pork sliders and green beans.

The catchy chorus from the old punk rock song "Should I Stay or Should I Go" runs through my head. My mind, desperate to escape the ravages of constant worrying about Ma, finds a different way to torture me. Kev's meeting with Spatick et al tugs at me, gnawing at my psyche.

I know the DMC job is the excuse Kennedy and I used to get Spatick, Kelly, and Blumenthal to give me what I want. But, what if that is the path I should really be on? What if the big house, bloated paycheck, and trappings of upper-class living are obstacles, keeping me from becoming the man I ought to be, the man the world needs me to be?

Ma, Dad, and I have never known luxury. Neither has Michelle nor Kennedy. We aren't pampered, nor materialistic. We are just decent people who love each other fiercely and strive every day, to the best of our abilities, to make the world a better place. And that is more than enough for us.

Standard psychological advice screams out at me, "Never make an important life decision under duress." Yeah, especially when your head isn't screwed on straight, and your heart, soul, and mind resemble a bowl of Shredded Wheat minus the milk. Hell, I don't even know why I am pondering all of this. It is an unwanted intrusion in my already overcrowded mind.

But I keep thinking about it just the same.

Intellectually it is a no brainer. Stay the course. Keep my family in the nice, big house on the water in one of the country's premier school districts. Look forward to our future, not back to the horrific attack on Ma and what might come of it. Continue my rewarding, life-saving work. Don't let my life be defined by tragedy but by hope.

If it were only that easy. I shake my head, desperate to jettison these crazy, unwanted thoughts.

They persist.

I push the cafeteria tray away from me and stare off into the distance, my eyes focused on nothing at all. My mind continues to churn.

I have always defined myself by how I handle adversity, by whether or not – or to what extent – I meet life's challenges. And by who I help – or hurt – in the process. It's why Kennedy and I fought back, hard, against every ruthless bully in Ossining who branded us worthless outsiders because we had the gall to show up unannounced in fourth grade. It's how I manage to keep an unmanageable, inoperable disease – my adrenaline-pumping pheochromocytoma – in check despite a career choice that should put me into attacks every hour of every working day.

Emotions run deep in me as does my adherence to a self-imposed moral code. Define your ideals. In my case, honor, integrity, and, okay at times, self-righteous rage and a thirst for vengeance. Live your life by those ideals. If it was just me, the choice would be easy, but I have a wife, a family to consider. What about their needs, their right to be happy?

I stare down at the sliders, skeptical there is any pork to speak of buried in the mound of bread and barbecue sauce before me. The awful truth is sinking in: no answers will be forthcoming today. Hell, I am lucky to identify the questions and to survive. Maybe I'll figure this all out another day. Maybe not.

I pick up the tray and walk over to the trashcan. My next case begins in thirty minutes. It is a tricky hiatal hernia with bowel poking through the morbidly obese patient's abdominal wall. I run over the case in my mind, trying to anticipate where difficulties can arise. Will I be able to use mesh or do I–

My phone dances in my pocket, imploring me to answer it before voicemail kicks in. I grab it without looking and answer the call.

Michelle is frantic. "Chris, Ma's waking up! Come quick."

§

I tear through the halls of Washington General,

dodging visitors, hospital employees, and a food cart. Three flights of stairs later I emerge on Ma's floor and hurry to her room.

Michelle and Dad are poised on each side of Ma, anxious to help her, yet uncertain what to do. Ma's eyes are open for the first time in nearly two weeks. Her head rolls around like a slowly spinning top. Her eyes catch mine. I see fear spark in them, then calm as she recognizes me. "Where am – Christopher! What's going on?"

Michelle and Dad peel off as I come to Ma's side. My heart is in my throat. I struggle to calm myself, to regain control. "I'm here, Ma! How do you feel?"

"I'm not sure. Hazy, out of it." She looks at her right hand and arm, IV tubing running to her inner elbow. "But I think it's getting better. What happened to me?"

Dad, Michelle, and I fill her in on the details of her attack, treatment, and recovery.

"I can't believe it. The last thing I remember was pulling off to help a stranded motorist in front of the botanical gardens...wait, I remember parts of the attack, fighting for my life. Oh, it was horrible! There were two of them."

"It's okay, honey. We're here, and that's all behind you now," Dad says as he squeezes her hand.

Mom smiles at each of us in turn. More fear flashes across her face before she dispels it. She senses something, but what? "Bill, Michelle, Christopher, I love all of you so, so much." She turns to Dad. "Bill, you have been the love of my life since the moment you started courting me in high school. You are such a great man, so caring, so strong. Always my protector and my champion." Mom smiles wistfully, placing two fingers over Dad's lips when he tries to speak. "It's been my honor to be your wife these last thirty-nine years."

Dad breaks through, "Mine too, Jackie. Each day I wake up with you by my side I pinch myself, amazed such a wonderful woman chose to be my beautiful bride." Dad leans in, kissing Ma softly on the lips before pulling back. He studies her face and rests his hand on her head. "You've been through a lot honey, I don't want you to overdo it. Maybe you should just rest quietly for a bit?

"No, I'm fine, Bill, and what I have to say can't wait."

Dad nods and backs away as Mom turns to my wife. "Michelle, I love you like one of my own. When Emily disappeared my heart was shattered. I would never know the joy of seeing my daughter happy again, of her raising her own family." Ma shakes her head with grief before brightening. "These last dozen years you have been the beautiful, sweet daughter that I missed." Ma chokes back the tears. Michelle's flow freely down her cheeks. "And just when I thought we couldn't be more blessed, you brought Christine and then James into our lives."

Ma wipes the tears away then embraces Michelle. As they part, Michelle speaks from the heart. "Jackie, I don't know what I would do without you. You pulled me through my mother's death, showed me how to move on, how to live my life with strength and dignity. Thank you. I love you too."

Ma nods with approval. She turns to me, tears welling up, her strength dissipating. "My dear, dear Christopher. You were just becoming a young man when Emily vanished." She becomes silent as emotion overcomes her. "Do you need some water, Ma?" I say. She smiles and takes the glass from me. Sipping it, she gathers her strength and takes a deep breath, then finds the St. Jude medallion hanging around my neck. Ma holds it up for me to grasp with her. "I was a broken woman, a lost cause after Emily. But you healed my heart." A pained look on her face, Ma struggles to continue, "You showed me how much love I still had to give." A tear-filled smile spreads across Ma's face. "You have brought your father and me such joy. We are so proud of who you have become." A faraway look comes into Ma's eyes as if she senses things we cannot see. She blinks twice, takes a breath, then presses on. "I know you will face many more challenges in your journey." She puts her hand and the medallion on my heart. "You will always be my saint of lost causes, Christopher. Know that I will be with you always." Tears run down my face as she continues, "I will help you, guide you, love you, no matter how difficult your life becomes."

I have so much to say, but my lips are frozen, paralyzed by the enormity of the moment. I sense our time together is growing short. Taking a deep breath, choked with emotion, I smile. "I love you so much, Ma and always will. I'm going to continue to do everything I can to make you proud of me, no matter what."

She looks at each of us in turn. Her face pales. "It will be hard when I'm gone, but I know you will care for each other so beautifully." We protest but Mom raises a hand to quiet us. Her words come with great effort now. "Do whatever you must to support each other... to move forward in your lives." Mom draws in a last deep breath. "Be beacons for this troubled world we live in...tell Christine and James how much Grandma loves them." Ma's eyes are half closed now, her voice weak. "I'll be watching over you all. God bless."

Mom collapses. Dad, Michelle, and I grab her, professing our love. We know we can't keep her with us even a moment longer, but we hold her tight and try just the same.

I hear footsteps crashing down the hall as the monitors scream their deadly messages. Her medical team tries valiantly, but it is not to be.

Dad, Michelle, and I are dazed and shaken. We huddle together, holding onto each other for support, knowing we will need all of our combined strength to survive this.

106

▷ Chapter 19 ◁

Tears stream forth as I read from 1 Corinthians 13:4-8. "Love is patient, love is kind. It does not envy...Love never fails..." I scan the crowd as I speak, taking solace there is not an empty seat or a dry eye in Our Lady of Mount Carmel. Old neighborhood friends, local merchants, volunteers from the soup kitchen and the parish, these and many others spill into the aisles to pay their respects to the most amazing woman any of us has ever known: Jacqueline Ann Ravello.

I step down from the lectern, bow, and cross myself and drag myself back to my seat.

Dad, Michelle, Kennedy, and I sit side by side, Christine and James interlaced between us. Father Domico delivers a heartfelt sermon, fighting back his own tears until the very end. Incense infuses the air.

A young man, whose life Mom helped turn back to God, sings *Ave Maria* beautifully to close out the mass.

We shuffle out of the church, our hearts shattered and torn, but buoyed by the beauty of the ceremony, by the bright summer sun, and the kind words of friends and strangers alike. Christine and James, tentative and fearful at first, hold hands and smile as the crowd works its way past us.

Both Doctor James and Doctor Hsu offer their deepest condolences, apologizing for failing to save Ma. I comfort them and ease their minds, then thank them for giving us a few last minutes to share heartfelt feelings with Mom.

Eventually, one of the pallbearers from the funeral home, a tall brown-haired man in a blue suit, prods us towards our cars and leads the procession to the Gate of Heaven cemetery in Valhalla.

Father Domico blesses and eulogizes Ma to close out the funeral. He recounts stories that capture her warmth, her wit, her passion, and her undying dedication to others.

I move slowly through it all, my arms and legs dead tree limbs swaying in the wind. I comfort Dad, Michelle, the kids, and Kennedy, trying to be strong the way Ma would want me to be. There are many poignant recollections, each easing the pain for a moment. But when her casket is lowered into the ground, the finality of saying goodbye to Ma is suffocating. I clutch the St. Jude medallion, longing for something, anything to ease the pain, to provide sense to her senseless passing.

One thought haunts me again and again, despite my efforts to banish it. Why couldn't I find a way to save my beloved mother from this horrible fate?

⊳ Chapter 20 ⊲

It is three a.m., six days after Mom's funeral. Michelle lays her head on my chest. Her arms envelop me, failing again in their quest to provide comfort. Lying in bed I stare at the ceiling, despondent and guilt-ravaged over my mother and what my state of mind is doing to Michelle.

"Honey, I'm so worried about you. What can I do to help?" The anguish in my beloved's voice is as tangible as the dried tears caked on her face. I search for answers or words of comfort, hoping to ease our pain or distract us from our suffering. Instead, a vise tightens around my heart as the depressing truth spills from my lips. "I don't know how I can make it through this. I'm so sad, so torn up inside."

Michelle kisses me tenderly, her hot, new tears mixing with my own. Her face slides next to mine.

Between tearful fits, she summons courage and wisdom and finds the only words with the power to save us. "We'll figure it out, Chris. Whatever it takes, whatever we need to go through, we'll find a way – together."

▸ Chapter 21 ◂

Thirteen days have passed since the funeral. Kennedy and my family are gathered at our house for Sunday dinner, our first since Mom's passing. It is the first of many firsts we need to pass through without her.

The Department of Surgery at Washington General graciously granted me an open-ended leave. Word had reached the powers that be about my lack of focus lately, about the patient I lost. This is an opportunity for them to cover their asses, to fully investigate my role in the patient's death as they consider what to do with me. Whatever the reasons, I am immensely grateful. I know I must heal myself before I can heal others. But how? I spend much of my time on edge, waiting for the next disaster to hit, the next attack of my disease to ravage me. Nightmares litter my evenings whether I sleep or am awake. In them, I kill patients by botching routine surgeries, or my poor choices lead to Ma's suffering and death. The epicenter of it all? Washington General.

The nightmares rob me of sleep, of my ability to cope, of peace. But not of anger. More and more I seethe with it, seeing vengeance as my only means of escape from this hell.

I shake my head, disgusted with myself for ruminating on these vile thoughts. I choose to get out of my own head, to enjoy my family and friend's company instead.

I smile at my father. "Dad, can you pass the potatoes, please?" I say with more effort than it should take.

"Sure, Chris. More steak as well?"

"No, I'm good, thanks."

"Michelle, you've outdone yourself again. This steak is amazing," Dad says between bites.

"Thank you, Bill. I'm glad you like it. We have plenty, so please take some home with you later."

"You need not ask twice," Dad says with a wink and a smile as Kennedy busies himself with cutting up Christine and James' steak for them. Two mouthfuls are the best we can hope for from them.

"Remember, kids, no mac and cheese until you finish all your steak," I say.

A frown takes over both their faces as they chew.

After dinner, we head into the living room.

Christine and James surround Grandpa on the couch while Michelle sits in the love seat and scrolls through Netflix. "Let's see what kind of movie we can make Grandpa suffer through tonight, huh, kids?" They howl their approval as Grandpa makes a silly face.

I am jealous of and at odds with my family. I know their lightheartedness, their moving forward with life is more mirage than reality. They must be hurting as much as I am. Still, I resent them and feel incredibly guilty and angry at myself because of it.

I chastise myself; enough is enough! This is no way to live. It's time to channel these negative feelings and thoughts, to transform them into purposeful, productive action.

"Honey, I'm going to sit inside with Kennedy and have some port. Anyone need anything?"

"No thanks, we're good," Michelle says absently as she stares at the screen before turning to me and smiling. "Don't be too long."

I gather two wine glasses and the aforementioned port, a 2008 late bottled offering from Taylor Fladgate, and join Kennedy at the kitchen's center island.

He eyes me carefully as I pour. "How are you holding up, Chris?" he says with concern.

"Not very well, I'm afraid," I reply before emptying my glass. "Unless alternating between nightmares and anger is the preferred way to be spending my days."

"Welcome to my life, buddy; the glamorous world of an NYPD detective," he says with sarcasm as he too empties his glass.

We eye each other carefully, wondering who will bring it up. I cave first. "You ready to pick up the scent on Ma's attackers, Kev?" Fury ignites my words, burning through them.

Kevin smiles. "I thought you'd never ask, Doctor Ravello. I've been keeping a bead on the low-life who knows Gonzalez and Damples. Ready to pounce when you are," he replies with satisfaction.

"How about tomorrow night?" I reply with intensity.

"Works for me, but what about the meeting with Spatick, Blumenthal, and Kelly? They want to reach an agreement with you before they let you start poking around."

"Shit, I forgot about that. How soon can you set that up?"

"These guys are anxious to speak with you, but they've got crazy schedules.... If I push hard I might be able to set it up for Wednesday or Thursday if I'm lucky."

"Damn, that's way too long to wait." I grind my teeth and shake my head in frustration. "NYPD dropped the frigging investigation weeks ago. I want to nail these fuckers now."

Kennedy leans forward onto his right elbow, his open hand rubbing his chin as he considers my words.

"The detective in me says we should wait on our investigating until after the Spatick meeting; it's the smart play." Kennedy's brow furrows, his jaw clenches. "But these bastards killed your mother, and I want payback as badly as you do. So, here's what we can do. I'll call Spatick and everyone else tomorrow. Push for meeting as soon as possible. Meanwhile, meeting or not, we work the low-life over tomorrow night for leads on Damples and Gonzalez. We ought to be able to pull that off without anybody finding out." I smile and nod in agreement. "But Chris, you've got to have an agreement in place with Spatick before we take it any further than that, agreed?"

I pour us each another glass of port, then clink mine against Kennedy's. "Well then, tomorrow night it is," I proclaim, fire filling my eyes.

▷ Chapter 22 ◁

Years of dedicated bodybuilding transformed Kevin Kennedy from the tall, lanky young man of our youth into a rock solid behemoth. No one in their right mind wants to be on the receiving end of his wrath, yet that is exactly where this street punk finds himself.

"Okay, Juan, you're running out of chances to save your scrawny ass from a world of pain," Kennedy bellows as the muscles in his forearms and biceps twitch in anticipation.

"It's like I been telling you, you got the wrong—"

Kennedy's right fist barrels into Juan's solar plexus, doubling him over. Kennedy grabs him by the hair and pulls Juan's face close to his own. "We can do this the easy way or the hard way, Juan. Makes no difference to me." Kennedy glances over at me and then bears down on Juan again. "We're currently doing things the easy way." Kennedy jerks his head my way. "But that will all change if he has to get involved."

The color drains from Juan's face as he looks over at me, poised behind a table, arranging surgical instruments.

I lift up a number 12 size scalpel. Light dances off its smooth, sharp blade as I hold it up and approach him. "We'd like to know the whereabouts of two associates of yours, a Mr. Teddy Gonzalez and Mr. Derrick Damples."

Kennedy steps aside, allowing me unfettered access. Juan sits in a wooden chair, arms tied behind his back, feet bound together and to the chair's base.

I run the edge of the blade along the left side of his windpipe, creating a trickle of blood.

He stares at me in horror, his eyes wide. "They'll fucking kill me if I tell you."

Kennedy speaks up, confirming our snitch's worse fear. "Juan, when this sick fuck is done with you, you'll wish you were dead."

I release the pressure on his neck, moving the scalpel in front of his left eye. "Seems like Juan is already deaf and dumb." My blade hovers a half inch away. Beads of sweat run down Juan's face as he tries to pull away. "Time we added blind to that list."

"Fuck! No! I'll spill. I'll spill."

I pull the blade back. "Wise choice, my friend."

"Gonzalez and Damples got a weekly meet in a

warehouse over on 139th and Malcolm X Boulevard. They'll be there Thursday night around eleven."

I begin gathering up my surgical instruments as Juan finishes filling us in on the details of the meeting. Kennedy stares at Juan with stone cold eyes.

"You breathe a word of this to anyone, ever, Juan, and we'll be back. And believe me, you do not want that."

Juan squeezes his eyes shut. "Got you, man. Never want to see you two again."

Kennedy pats him on the cheek. "That a boy, Juan. You're getting the hang of this. No need to get up, we'll show ourselves out." Kennedy looks down at Juan's pants and makes a sniffing gesture with his nose. "Oh, and Juan. I'd probably get a change of clothes if I was you."

§

"Not my proudest moment with a scalpel," I say with regret. "Don't want to have to do that again anytime soon." Kennedy and I barrel along Gun Hill Road in the Bronx. It's a hellhole of a neighborhood, a far cry from the place it used to be when Ralph Lauren, Robert Klein, and others grew up here. We're heading home.

"Very convincing though, Doctor Ravello. You

literally had that guy shitting in his pants," Kennedy booms.

"Wonderful," I say with a sarcastic smile. "Nice to know I have something to fall back on if a career in medicine doesn't work out, and right now that's not looking too good."

A grin stretches across Kev's face. "I wouldn't quit the day job just yet, buddy." Kennedy's laughter reverberates off the interior of his ancient Honda Civic. A few moments later his face becomes deadly serious, and his eyes turn into narrow slits. "Score a victory for us tonight, Chris. But Thursday is gonna be the hard part. In the morning you've got the meeting I set up for you with Spatick, Kelly, and Blumenthal. That night we've got the Gonzalez/Damples meet Juan just told us about." Kennedy takes a deep breath, exhales, and twists his head to work the tension out of his neck. "We got away with one tonight, but we can't push it any further. Thursday night is our chance to get the goods on Gonzalez and Damples and arrest them. No way that works without you onboard with NYPD by then."

I nod my head in acknowledgment. "I hear you loud and clear, Kev. No matter what, I've got to come to an agreement with Spatick during that meeting."

▷ Chapter 23 ◁

"**Y**ou've got nothing to worry about, buddy. You'll have them eating out of your hand in no time," Kennedy chuckles, one arm draped over my shoulder as he pats my chest.

"I wish I had your confidence, Kev." My eyes nervously scan the long hallway for eavesdroppers as I stand poised in front of the O'Toole conference room. "But, telling the governor, the mayor, and the police commissioner I'll run the DMC for them, and then blowing them off when this case is over? I work at a city-run hospital. You realize how badly these three guys can fuck me if I cross them?!"

Kennedy slides in front of me, his massive hands massaging the base of my neck, between my shoulders. "You're gonna be fine, Chris. These guys have been playing it casually, but they want you badly. The DMC is a frigging mess, so their necks are on the chopping block.

They need you to ride in on your white horse with your stethoscope and medical bag to save their asses."

"Great, no pressure there." My voice trails off as I turn my head from Kennedy and say a silent prayer. I hear rumblings coming from the police commissioner's office at the far end of the hallway.

Kennedy turns my head forward and pats my right cheek. "You're holding all the cards, my friend. No matter what happens, don't forget that," he says with a smile. Before I can reply, he spins me around awkwardly and pushes me towards the conference room door.

Off balance, I do a one-eighty as I stagger backward, catching myself just before my back hits the door. I straighten up and smooth my sports jacket arms and lapel. As my eyes rise up to meet Kennedy's, a smirk spreads across both our faces, and Kennedy flashes me a confident thumbs up. I wink at him, then disappear through the conference room door.

Spatick, Kelly, and Blumenthal are jarred by my sudden entry. Their animated conversation and hand waving come to an abrupt end. I recognize each of them from press conferences I have seen on television. Spatick, a well built, brown-haired man in a blue suit, breaks away from the others, rising to shake my hand.

"A pleasure to meet you, Doctor Ravello. Detective Kennedy speaks highly of you."

Commissioner Kelly's face fills with disdain, Blumenthal's with curiosity as they shift in their seats.

"Thank you, Governor. It's a pleasure to be here."

The others rise as Spatick makes the introductions. Blumenthal's handshake and head nod are polite and perfunctory. Kelly's is rough, aggressive, domineering. As we sit down, I size up the diverse and divisive trio before me. Kennedy's bio and assessment of each echo in my mind.

Kelly, a rough looking, pock-faced man in his late fifties. Born in Coney Island and reared on ill-tempered streets in a predominantly Irish section of Boston, he rocketed through the ranks of the police department. If I cross him, he's as likely to beat the crap out of me in some dark, deserted alley as he is to have me arrested on whatever charges he can make stick. Can I ever find common ground with Kelly, earn his respect, if I choose to work for him?

Blumenthal, a tall erudite, who possesses an air of even temperedness. He made his fortune as a real estate developer, then turned his attention to public service. Working with an impartial, fair-minded observer like him is ideal, but Blumenthal is a man of immense wealth and power. There is likely much more to him than I see at first blush.

Spatick, the consummate politician. Gracious and endearing one moment, haughty, aloof, prickly the next. Spatick warrants the most caution. He will find me as likable as I am useful to him: no more, no less.

During his ascent to the governorship, Spatick lay waste to his opponents. His calling card? No holds barred, vicious attacks on any who dare to oppose him. With the full power of his office at his disposal, there's no telling what he will do to me if I cross him.

Tightness fills my chest. Screw up this meeting and I am shut out of the investigation into Mom's killers. Promise I will run their DMC and then renege, and these heads of government and law enforcement will find a way to take my head and hide as payment.

I need a way to survive this blindfolded march across a minefield.

Spatick speaks first. "I assume Detective Kennedy filled you in on the substance of our conversation?" An insincere smile and hollow, soulless blue eyes fill his face.

I shift uncomfortably in my seat, crossing my legs. Here we go. "Yes, yes he has, sir."

"Good. We're prepared to grant your unusual request, to allow your participation in the investigation of your mother's attackers." Spatick's tone is cautious, controlled. "In exchange, we require certain assurances from you." Chunks of earth explode in front and to the sides of me as I hold my ground, wary.

"...such as?"

"We'll consider this investigation an unofficial tryout of sorts."

"Please don't commit to anything at this point, sir." Kelly fights to rein in his rancor. "We need to keep our options open regarding Doctor Ravello."

Spatick glares at Kelly, driving a bayonet through his skull. He turns to Blumenthal, ready for battle but finds none.

"If your investigation is fruitful and your performance satisfactory, you will accept the role of division chief for our fledgling Division of Medical Crimes. How does that sound, Doctor Ravello?" A bullet whizzes by my head, grazing my ear. I step forward and feel a mine engage beneath my foot.

"Uh, that's quite an honor, sir. But how would I run the DMC with such little investigative experience? I'm a doctor, not a police officer."

"An easily remedied issue, Doctor." A serpent tongue springs forth from Spatick's face. "We will send you to the police academy, and upon graduation, you'll work in the field a few weeks, then take over the DMC as a detective third grade. Detective Kennedy will make an excellent partner for you, and I'm sure he'll appreciate the valuable experience and bump in his pay."

Kelly grits his teeth and rolls his eyes to the heavens as his right hand mangles his face. Blumenthal looks on in silence, as if witnessing a car accident he is powerless to prevent.

Great, I think. Spatick is a real piece of work. Not only is he using Ma to try and back me into a corner, now he's making my best friend's promotion dependent on me as well. What's next for this guy? Does he want to hold Michelle and the kids hostage till I agree? Maybe find a way to deny Dad his detective's pension till I see the light?! Geez, it's going to be interesting, I'm sure, working with this guy.

"Would running the DMC be a full-time endeavor?" I say sheepishly, before brightening my tone, "or would I consult on an as-needed basis, continuing on with my medical practice until called upon?"

Spatick's eyes grow large. His jaw clenches then releases. "I want to be perfectly clear on this, Doctor. This is a full-time position. Your services will be needed throughout New York State."

Spatick sees concern flash across my face. Extensive travel, loss of time with Michelle, Christine, and James. I'd rather not make such a sacrifice if I can help it. Sensing he is losing me, Spatick backpedals. "On the bright side, two-thirds of the state's population is in the New York City Metropolitan area, so many of the crimes are perpetrated within the five boroughs, Long Island, and Westchester County. As a result, the DMC's main office is located in Midtown Manhattan, in

126

Detective Kennedy's precinct, the 1-7. " Spatick flashes his fake smile again.

"I see." I ponder the mine beneath my foot, then flash back to Ma's body as they lowered it into her grave. My anger and determination swell. The lowlifes who killed Ma need to pay, and I need to be the one to bring them to justice. But there is even more at stake, a greater good to achieve beyond mere vengeance. Ma's last words ring in my ears. "Be beacons for this troubled world we live in...."

I nod my head and look at Kelly, then Blumenthal, before my gaze comes to rest on Spatick. My eyes, so unlike his, blaze like a raging forest fire.

The words burst forth. "Count me in, sir."

§

"You said what?!" Kennedy asks in astonishment.

" 'Count me in' were my exact words," I say in a whisper.

Kennedy tilts his massive head back and whistles, the sound ricocheting off the car's interior. "Working together will be great, Chris, you know that. But what happened to our plan, to stringing them along without making a commitment? After all your years of schooling and residency, is running the DMC really what you want?"

I am a doer, not a ponderer. I often leap before

I look. My proclamation with Spatick was one such moment. I shift my lower jaw to one side, then the other. "What choice did I have? You told me Monday night I needed an agreement in place with Spatick before the Damples/Gonzalez meeting so we can bust them. Spatick had me cornered. I had to commit. Besides, the more I hear Ma's last words in my head, the more I'm convinced she wanted me to do something like this."

Kennedy's head bobs back and forth as he takes it all in, eyes fixated on the winding road ahead. "I see your point, Chris. I just figured you'd get them to agree by stringing them along. But what the hell is Michelle going to say about this?! She on board with it?"

The color drains from my face. I was too caught up in what Ma had said to me and the moment. My approach seemed like the perfect solution, my only path to success. Now I'm not so sure. "God I hope so. We didn't exactly discuss that part of things."

Kennedy turns and looks my way, ignoring the road, his right forefinger waving in front of me. "Well, don't pin this on me. I ain't afraid of too many people in this world, buddy, but when Michelle's mad, she's on that short list."

My hand reflexively rubs my jaw as I assess the situation. "Yeah, me too. She did say, 'Whatever it takes, we'll get through this.' I hope this is what she meant." I hold Kennedy's gaze. "I'll talk to her tonight. In the meantime, we've got to keep this under wraps, okay?"

Kennedy turns and studies the road before him. "Sure thing, cowboy. Maybe I ought to lend you my bullet proof vest though, in case things don't go so well," he says with a sarcastic laugh as I sink down into my seat.

▸ Chapter 24 ◂

A white Lenox vase flies past me, narrowly missing my head as I duck. It crashes against the bedroom wall next to me and shatters on impact. Shards of ivory fly in every direction as white lilies slump to the floor. I stand in the doorway, uncertain if I should move forward or flee.

"You told them, what?! Are you crazy?" Michelle screams at me. She is a crazed animal, desperate to inflict more damage.

So much for the honest approach.

"They had me backed into a corner. What was I going to do?" I say, palms pinned to my sides in surrender.

"For starters, tell them this is a big decision, I need to discuss it with my wife." Her nostrils flare, smoke pours out of them. Her eyes scan the area, hungry to find something else to hurl my way. I decide it's time to act before she does. I take three quick steps forward, blocking her from turning an array of antiques on her dresser into missiles.

"Uh, yeah...that's probably what I should have done. But last week you said, 'Whatever it takes, whatever we need to go through, we'll find a way.'" I reach out to touch my wife.

Michelle's eyes bulge as she swats my hands away. Lunging forward, her fists pound on my chest, then her head collapses into me as she half screams, half cries, "Together. I said whatever we need to go through, we'll find a way – together." Tears soak through my shirt. I look up, startled to find Christine in our doorway. I have no idea what she witnessed, but I see her fingers at her lips, the bewilderment in her eyes. Silently she cries. I am torn, uncertain who to comfort now.

"Daddy, I'm scared," she says in a small voice.

Michelle, stunned, pulls back, her eyes a mess of mascara, her face awash with guilt. My eyes dart from Christine to Michelle and back again. Three strides and I am kneeling by Christine. "It's okay, kiddo. Everything is all right. Let me get you back to bed." As I carry my girl down the hall, Michelle quickly exits the bedroom. Her head turned away from us in embarrassment, Michelle waves to Christine, whose chin rests on my shoulder. "I'm sorry, baby girl, Mommy needs to cool off. I'll be back later after you're asleep."

The front door opens and closes as I tuck Christine

under her pink comforter and Tinkerbell throw. I hug Christine, then kiss her cheek as I rub her head.

"Why did Mommy leave?" she wonders.

My eyes search Christine's, finding innocence and fear. She has never seen Michelle like this. Neither have I. "It's okay, honey. Sometimes adults have disagreements and get real mad. Mommy went for a drive to calm down so she and I can talk later."

A quizzical look on Christine's face gives way to understanding. She shakes her pointer finger at me. "Daddy, did you get in trouble again with Mommy?" Nervous, pent up tension erupts from my belly as laughter. "Yes I did, sweetie. Yes, I did. But Daddy will make it better later. Now, try to go back to sleep."

§

I look down at my watch. "Shit." I was supposed to meet Kennedy twenty minutes ago and go over the plan for tonight. What the hell am I gonna do?

As much as I don't want to get back into it with Michelle, I need her to look after the kids for me. Worry creeps into my mind. This is not like Michelle. She's been gone over an hour and there's no telling when she'll be back. I dial her cell, but it kicks over to voicemail immediately. A text gets me nowhere as well. Crap. Now what? I can't go out looking for her.

Dad.

Maybe she's at his house. I call him, frantic. "No, I haven't heard from her, Son. Tell you what, I'll come over so you can go out and look for her, okay?"

"That'd be great, Dad. I'll see you soon. Bye." I call around to Michelle's closest friends, but none of them have seen her. I am sick with worry.

A vague pain, nothing more than an annoyance at first, flares up in my chest. Over the next thirty seconds, it spreads to my arms and up to my neck. My face feels flush. A minute more and the pain is an ice pick in my chest. Sweat drips off of my forehead and face as I struggle to catch my breath. I don't need to look in the mirror or check my blood pressure to know what's going on. It's what Doctor Jacobs warned me about the other day.

My disease, the damn pheochromocytoma is rearing its ugly head once again.

My body is succumbing to the plague of stress, guilt, sorrow, and anger that consumes me. I struggle to take slow, deep breaths, to calm myself despite the pain. Absent an emergency room, it's the only way I know how to control the pheo at moments like these.

Minutes drag by. My condition teeters out of control. I become lightheaded, faint.

Then it happens.

Gradually, as imperceptibly as it began, the adrenaline coursing through my body recedes and my pain diminishes. A few minutes later the episode passes completely.

Sitting on the stairs, my head is hunched forward between my knees as I recover from the attack. My hands are still locked in a white knuckle grip behind my head. I nearly jump through the ceiling as the doorbell chimes. I approach the door, gathering myself, and pull it open. "Oh, hey Dad," I say with feigned nonchalance.

"Hi, Son. Any word?"

"Not yet, I'm afraid." I wave him towards a seat in the living room and fill him in on the fight.

Dad eyes me warily, nodding his head, but does not speak.

"So I don't know what to do. I've got to find her, Dad, but I'm also supposed to meet Kennedy–"

The front door springs forward. Michelle strides through it and comes into view.

I jump up and head towards her. "Thank God you're all right, honey. I was so worried."

Michelle's eyes rivet on mine, freezing me in place. "Don't." She softens as she spots Dad, confusion filling her face. "Bill, what are you doing here?"

He looks at me dispassionately, then back at Michelle. "Chris wanted me to come over so he could go out looking for you. Guess I better be on my way."

Guilt flashes across her face. "No, please stay, Bill." She glances at me, her anger dissipating, then back at Dad. "I can really use someone to talk to right now, and

134

Chris has somewhere he needs to be, don't you, *honey*?" I welcome the words despite not understanding their context. Is she thinking of me and where I need to be, or does she just want me the hell out of the house?

"Yeah, that's right," I say with an ignorant nod.

"Join me for some coffee, Bill?"

More awkward glances. "Sure thing. I'll pull up a chair."

That settles that, I think as I head out the door. Michelle is safely home, and I'm off to meet Kennedy. No telling how Michelle and Dad's conversation will go – or how big a firestorm I'm in for later.

⯈ Chapter 25 ⯇

"He's been like this since childhood, Michelle. The hero-idealist ridiculously focused at times on one thing to the exclusion of everything else." Bill Ravello shakes his head and looks down at his coffee. "As much as we'd all like to see it, I'm afraid he's not about to change." Bill fights back a wave of grief. "Especially while he's hell bent on catching Jackie's killers."

Michelle nods in somber acknowledgment. Grief and guilt torment her. Regret and anger claw at her already raw insides. "I just don't know what to do, Bill. Chris needs me so badly now and..." Her hands cover her mouth, then smear away tears as they spill down the sides of her cheeks. "I really messed up tonight. Oh gosh, and Christine saw it. She saw her mother behaving like a banshee, hurling things at her father." Michelle's face collapses in her hands, her tears in full force.

"There, there, dear," Bill says, a hand rising to her shoulder in comfort. An involuntary laugh spills from his lips. "In thirty-nine years of marriage, Jackie and I had some doozies ourselves. She damn near took my head off with a frying pan once. Chris was six at the time. I was pushing her hard to get out of the Bronx, putting the full court press on her about how we needed to make a better life for the kids in the suburbs and get Emily away from some bad influences. The Bronx was all Jackie had known at that point, and she wanted none of it." Bill's hand rises, feeling its way through his hair. "Look right here; got the scar to prove it."

Her guilt assuaging, Michelle lifts her head and stares at the jagged, three-inch scar. "Oh, my, how terrible. How come I never noticed that before?"

"Good thing for Chris you don't have Jackie's pinpoint aim." Bill laughs heartily now, the reminiscence a welcome relief.

A smile fills Michelle's face as she shakes her head and wipes away her tears. "No one can ever accuse the Ravellos of being pacifists or wallflowers."

A shy smile overtakes Bill's face as he sips his coffee. He reaches out and pats Michelle's hand. "Truer words have never been spoken."

Time drifts by, comfortable small talk and anecdotes filling the minutes, before the topic again turns serious.

"Michelle, take it from a veteran of the NYPD,

this plan of Chris' to take over the DMC is lunacy." Bill looks around at the wonderfully appointed kitchen with outstretched arms. "Look at all you have here. The two of you have worked so hard, sacrificed so much, you deserve all of this, not living on a detective's pay in a sketchy neighborhood. What is that son of mine thinking?"

Michelle smiles, her words filled with pride. "Bill, your son has the most amazing heart and soul. He is so selfless, so determined to do good in the world." She blinks a few times before continuing. "It's what I love and adore most about him." The smile runs away from her face. "Jackie's death has torn Chris up. He can't sleep, couldn't function at work. He's a zombie around the house. I know it's only been two weeks, but I'm worried he won't ever be the same if he goes back to Washington General, back to the way things were."

Michelle pauses and draws an involuntary breath. "The only thing that brings him comfort, brings him back to himself, is when he's tracking down who did this to your wife. To everyone else, it seems like it's all about vengeance. But I know Chris. It's not. Vengeance is just a piece of it, the first phase of him working through it all. It's about getting closure for Jackie and all of us. It's about Chris dedicating himself to doing what he feels is right."

Michelle's smile returns in full force. "I'm sure he believes running the DMC will help others avoid the same fate we are all suffering through." Michelle puts a hand on Bill's. "I'm not saying I'm convinced or on board with this. Just look how I acted tonight as proof, but if I'm to love your son the way he needs me to, I have to be open to whatever he asks of me."

<h1 style="text-align:center">▷ Chapter 26 ◁</h1>

"**K**ev, I'm all set to meet up. Are you at the old DAK furniture warehouse on Malcolm X Boulevard and 139th?"

"Yeah, bud," Kennedy says in a whisper. "I've been here since 9:30. Nobody's gone in yet. Where the hell you been?"

I glance at my watch as the Firebird carves its way through heavy traffic: 11:14 p.m. The summer air blasts across my face: thick, oppressive. "Trouble with Michelle. She flipped out when I told her about the meeting with Spatick. Look, I'm just passing the Fordham Road exit on 87. I should be there in like ten minutes."

"Okay, I'll wait. Nothing happening – hold on – I see about five guys, including Damples and Gonzalez getting out of a black Mercedes and an old, beat up, silver Nissan Sentra." Kennedy compresses his massive frame against the Honda's driver side bucket seat. The gear shifter bites into his right leg as he peers at the motley crew exiting the two cars. "They're entering the warehouse on the north side of 139th street. I'm in my car across the street. Get here as fast as you can."

I shoot past Yankee Stadium and the Bronx Terminal Market, weaving erratically through traffic. I cut off a taxi cab, then a lumbering bus as I exit at 138th Street/Madison Avenue Bridge. Only in New York do you find this much traffic this late at night! The moon's crooked reflection dances off the Harlem River below as I accelerate across the bridge. Almost there. Gas pedal one with the floor, I blow through the traffic light at 138th Street and Fifth Avenue and barrel down the narrow side street. Parked cars litter the sides of the road. Suddenly, a red Saab lurches out of a driveway a few feet ahead on my right. No way to avoid impact. I cut left, then back right as I pass it, metal grinding against metal, sparks flying everywhere. "Shit! Out of the way," I scream as I pound on the car horn. Pedestrians scatter for cover as I skid through the intersection, turning right onto Malcolm X Boulevard. A heartbeat later, tires screeching, rubber burning into the asphalt, I jump the curb, missing a parking meter by inches, as I careen onto 139th street heading east. Kennedy's car is up ahead. I slam on the brakes, the Firebird skidding to a halt alongside his car.

Kennedy mouths, "What the fuck?!" as I throw the

car into reverse and park behind him. I cut the engine and yank out the keys. We meet at the front of my car. "Subtle, real subtle," he says with annoyance. "Come on, let's get in there before the whole neighborhood knows we're here."

§

"We've got no idea what the layout is in there," Kennedy says as he rams two short, blunt metal rods into the lock, frees the tumblers, and eases the door open. "Which means stay alert, stay quiet, and we might just stay alive," he says in a whisper. Stone-faced and still, I nod, then follow Kennedy into the unknown.

Glimpses of light spill through a few windows high above us. The slivers of illumination pierce the darkness that cloaks us as they cast eerie, irregular shadows. Large, sturdy, smooth crates– all sealed – jigsaw before us. I pull out my cell phone and activate the flashlight, taking care to avoid lighting up anything that attracts attention to us. Kennedy and I scramble, then huddle behind a crate. Long vents run horizontally along the crates at two-foot intervals. In between the vents are labels indicating "Hospital Supplies." Kennedy and I hold our breath. Muffled sounds, almost spent, stagger to my ears, their messages indecipherable. Moments crawl by.

I tap Kennedy on the shoulder. "We're too far

away, Kev. We need to get closer somehow." He nods, then darts behind an adjacent container. Peering around it, studying what lies ahead, he strains to make out details. The men we seek are gathered in a circle of light about twenty-five feet away. A sliver of light cuts across Kennedy's chiseled face as he mouths "Follow me" and waves his hand. On his heels I scramble forward, in silence, I hope. Sounds coalesce into voices as we close in on our prey.

"Of all the old people out there, you two fuck heads had to pick one with some stones, some fight in her! Or are you two just bigger pussies than I thought?" yells the tall, dark-skinned man in the business suit in the center of the group. His anger slams into Gonzalez and Damples like storm-ravaged waves against a battered shore.

"Well, how was we supposed to know?" Gonzalez replies. "It's not like we picking and choosing, boss. We just grab whoever's stupid enough to come along."

Unmoved, their boss continues. "Yeah, well who looks stupid now? Fucking story's all over the news. Bitch's husband is a retired detective, her son, some big shot surgeon – at Washington General of all fucking places! The news said everybody in Little Italy loved her, so there are eyes all over, thanks to you two."

The hairs on my neck stand at attention as I realize they are talking about me, about Mom, and about Dad.

I peer around the crate, catch two other men, armed no doubt, standing on each side of their boss.

Damples speaks up. "What you want us to do now, man? Take out the husband? The doc?"

"Are you fuckin' kidding me, Derrick? Heat's all over this one. No way in hell we get close enough now to pop either one of them. You try it, the cops will be up our asses, big time." The boss shakes his head, anger written across his face. "No, we just need to lay low a while, let everyone forget about her."

I'm pissed, ready to tear these scumbags apart. I look at Kennedy for guidance, a plan on how to move on these guys. He puts a hand up, lowers it down indicating sit tight, be patient. *Sure, easy for him*, I think to myself. I stay in a crouch, like a caged animal, waiting to pounce, but wary.

My insides are knotted in conflict. I need to act, need to make these pieces of shit pay for what they did to Mom. But charging in without a plan, getting killed, accomplishes nothing. We need evidence on these guys. But we also need an exit strategy. I look over at my partner. Kennedy's a cop, a detective first grade. He's got ten years of this shit under his belt and a gun in his holster. Me, I'm just a pissed off doc in a navy blazer, with only a few tricks up my sleeve, none of which may matter here. I've got no idea how to approach this situation, no idea what the plan is – if there's a plan. Kennedy and I were supposed to meet earlier to sort that out, but the fiasco with Michelle robbed us of the time to do that. I grind my teeth. I peer ahead, straining to see inside the lit circle. One thing I do know, there's five of them and only two of us. Hell bent on vengeance or not, I don't like these odds.

Gonzalez pipes in, "I thought those clients of yours, they need them organs like yesterday, boss. They ain't gonna like no delays." The boss grabs Gonzalez by the shirt, pulls his pockmarked face up to his and spits out his reply. "So now you're the brains of this operation, Gonzalez?!" He throws his underling backward like an unwanted rag doll as he continues, "Shut the fuck up before we cut the organs we need outta you." The boss rubs his hand against his chin as Gonzales scrambles to his feet, moving farther away. "I just need a minute to figure this out, figure what we do next."

Kennedy studies the situation intently, nods to himself, and reaches towards his pants pocket for his radio–

BANG, BANG, BANG!

The sound reverberates from inside the container I'm crouching behind. The blood drains from my face. Kennedy's too as we jump back. Shit!

Their leader reacts. "What the fuck?" His men grab their guns as we hide behind the container. I look at Kennedy with panic, confusion. What now?

The answer comes, seconds later, from behind us.

Click.

The unmistakable sound of a gun being cocked. Even a doctor knows what that sounds like.

§

Cold hard steel burrows into the back of my head. Beams of light come from the side, stabbing my eyes.

"Well, well, what do we have here?" I glimpse a burly, bearded man with a small, silver revolver before the light blinds me. He steps back as his partner draws his own gun on Kennedy and blinds him with his flashlight.

"Looks like a couple of trespassers. Let's see what the boss wants to do with them. Come on you two, this way."

Two guys, two guns, and blinded by the light. No choice but to comply.

We trudge forward in silence, through a maze of identical crates, the flashlight's rays scattering the darkness before us. We reach the clearing. The ringmaster and his henchman stand poised, their bodies bathed in the bright light of an electric lantern that rests on the floor between them. "Rodriguez, turn off that fucking flashlight so I can see." Recognition flashes in their leader's eyes as the four of us step forth. A sinister smile spreads across his face.

"Your ears must have been burning, Doctor Ravello. How good of you to join us." His attention turns to my partner. "And who is this neanderthal you brought along?"

Kennedy's neck veins bulge as he scans the three before us. His eyes narrow. "Detective Kevin Kennedy out of the 1-7," he grumbles. "And you are?"

The criminal scans the crowd around him. "I am the one who runs this operation, who provides our wealthy clientele with the organs they so desperately need." He looks squarely at Kennedy and me. "I'd prefer to keep my name secret, so you may call me The Facilitator."

"Sounds like a frigging cartoon character. Where's your cape, dickhead?" Kennedy smiles. He balls his hands into fists, then releases them. Gonzalez and Damples move forward, hands raised, ready to pounce. Their boss waves them off, his smile morphing into a cold stare.

I scan our surroundings. Three men in front of us, two behind. The lantern throws off about fifteen feet of light, beyond that darkness pervades. Gonzales and Damples, to our left: young, inexperienced, stupid, and apparently unarmed. No threat there. The two bruisers behind us are harder to assess, probably well trained. One thing is certain: Kennedy and I have to figure a way out of this. Fail and we're dead men.

"So, Facilitator, how is it you know me but I have no idea who you or your little band of merry morons are?" I interject.

The smile returns.

"Ah, but I'm sure you know at least these two, Doctor Ravello," the dark-skinned leader says as he waves his hand towards Gonzalez and Damples. "Why else would you be here?" He turns towards the men. "Refresh my memory, Gonzalez, was it you or Damples who waved down the now deceased Mrs. Ravello on that fateful afternoon?" The grin widens, begging me to tear it off his face. I need to keep him talking, create an opening for Kev and me.

"You've got me there. But it begs the question, what the hell are you doing hanging out with the likes of Gonzalez and Damples?" I jerk my thumb towards them as I continue my false bravado. "These guys are two-bit players. You strike me as a tad bit more ambitious."

Gonzalez and Damples are fuming now, two bulls ready to charge out of their gates.

"How perceptive of you, Doctor. The boss sneers with delight. "Gonzalez and Damples are but two of a host of freelancers my organization employs for grunt work. They provide us with a fresh supply of local citizens. Other associates of mine harvest their organs and send them on their way to wealthy benefactors. It's a delightfully lucrative business."

"So, that's what you had in mind for my mother that day, using her as a live organ donor?" My face twists into an angry glare.

"I'm afraid so, Doctor." His face assumes the shape of mock sorrow. "Nothing personal, you realize."

Lasers shoot out of my eyes, turning the lot of them into ashes.

"There's much more to it, of course." He ponders his next move, nods towards Kennedy, then me. "Just you two here tonight, or are we expecting others?"

"Just us two," I blurt out before Kennedy can object.

"Well, that makes it easy. We can kill the both of you and dump your bodies without any of it tracing back to us." He pauses, sizing me up, then slowly flexes his shoulders and neck. He rubs his chin as he stares at us, deep in thought. "Easy enough but such a waste. I have a proposition for you, Doctor Ravello, a way for you to save yourself and your partner."

His eyes narrow. Mine do the same.

"Come join us."

"Excuse me?"

"Join us."

"Are you frigging crazy?! You just killed my mother and you want me to join forces with you?" I turn and look at his goons. "If it wasn't for your friends here, I'd be choking the life out of you right now."

"How courageous and fearsome of you, Doctor, but not very practical, I'm afraid. The fact is, Kennedy and you will be dead in a few minutes unless you agree to my proposal."

This guy is out of his mind. But I need him to keep

talking till I catch him off guard. I look at Kennedy, then back at him.

"What do you have in mind?" I say with a huff.

"Ah, now you're talking..." He draws in a deep, calming breath and slowly exhales. "We kill the few for the benefit of the many. The victims provide us with a fresh supply of kidneys, hearts, lungs, livers, corneas, bone marrow...well, you get the idea, Doctor. Each single death provides many more with life."

"How noble of you to provide such much-needed work." I turn to Kennedy. "Kev, these guys are up for sainthood, don't you think?"

He smiles. "No question. I'm honored just to be in their presence."

Our dark-skinned friend presses on, undeterred. "Above it all, are we?" He throws his head back and laughs. "You'll be surprised, no doubt, to find colleagues of yours already among our ranks. They too had ethical concerns in the beginning, but no more." The laughing stops. The Facilitator fixes his gaze on me. "You'll find the work, harvesting organs, easy enough, Doctor Ravello." His sales pitch intensifies. "In the beginning, our operation was small, the profits modest. But now we have more business than we can handle, which is where you come in. We'll make you rich beyond your wildest dreams, and no one will be the wiser since your day job serves as the perfect cover." He looks at Kennedy, then back at me. "We'll put Detective

Kennedy to good use, find a way for the two of you to continue your partnership."

"And all I need to do is kill for you in exchange," I reply with intensity.

"We'll carry out our plans with or without you, Doctor. Innocents will die, to be sure. But their blood is on our hands, not yours. We are the ones masterminding this. You will be but a cog in the wheel, a good man following orders."

"Sounds like the same reasoning the Nazis used to convince their men to carry out atrocities." I shake my head from side to side. "No thanks. I'd rather die with honor than serve without it."

The boss' head shakes. "As you wish. Joe, Frank, bring them to their knees before me."

Kennedy and I make eye contact as we are driven forward. "You heard him. Move it!"

We stagger towards The Facilitator, our fate sealed by my refusal. I think of Michelle, of Christine and James, and of Dad. My heart aches.

"On your knees, you idealistic fools. Prepare to meet your maker."

Kennedy and I swallow hard. Joe and Frank jam their guns between our shoulder blades. They force us down, like lambs being slaughtered. The henchmen raise their guns to our heads and ready them. Their boss looks at us, his eyes filled with disdain. "Any last words?" We stare back in silence. "Very well." The boss nods to his men. "Finish them."

The moment unfolds as if in slow motion. Three more bangs from the nearby container pierce the air, startling everyone, including the thugs trying to shoot us. Two hammers fall, propelling the bullets forward. Joe and Frank jerk in surprise as Kennedy and I pivot, taking their legs out from under them. The shots fly wildly. One whizzes by Damples' ear, the other pierces Gonzalez in the chest. He falls to the ground, motionless, dead. Spooked, Damples scatters into the darkness. Kennedy takes Joe out with a single gunshot to the neck before he can return fire, then tackles Frank as he tries to get to his feet. The two exchange blows, but Frank is no match for Kennedy, who knocks him out with a right cross to the head, then grabs his gun and begins cuffing him.

I lunge for the boss as he hurriedly pulls a .38 caliber revolver out of his jacket and thrusts the barrel towards my head. I twist in midair as he fires. The odor of spent fireworks and charcoal sprays across my face as the shot rips past me, grazing my left chest. My head slams into his abdomen and chest, propelling him backward as the gun flies out of his hand, sliding behind him. I jam my right hand in his face, slamming his head backward onto the concrete floor as I power forward, desperate to reach the gun first. My feet trample over his motionless legs, groin, and chest. Almost past him.

Just a few more feet to the gun. Another second or two at most. Suddenly his hands shoot up and grab my legs, tripping me up as they pull me down. I strike the floor hard. I flail and claw at the concrete as he drags me backward, across his body.

Our grimy, sweat-soaked faces meet in grim determination. His right hand disappears into his jacket. A moment later a steel blur lunges towards me. I strike his arm hard, knocking it back as my momentum carries me forward. His left arm pushes me, face first, towards the floor as he scrambles, then jumps on top of my back. We tumble, rolling over and over. Kennedy, finished with Frank, turns towards us, and rises to his feet. We come to a crashing halt, the boss on his back, my upper back on his chest. He thrusts his knife across the front of my throat, using me as a shield, as Kennedy draws a bead on us.

"Drop it, Detective, or Ravello dies." I thrust my elbow back at him, missing the mark as he pulls out from under me and gets to his knees. I struggle to free myself, then freeze as he jams the knife against my windpipe and adjusts his position behind me.

I yell, "Take the shot, Kev," as I feel the boss' breath on my neck. Kennedy has the power to save himself, to take out this bastard. I need him to do it. "Don't worry about me, I'll be fine."

"Detective Kennedy is far too experienced to take such a risky shot. Aren't you, Detective?"

Anger and pain etch themselves into Kennedy's face as he assesses the situation, searching for an opening. His eyes meet mine, then The Facilitator's. Resignation washes over him. Kevin lowers the gun as both our faces collapse.

We were so close to turning the tables on these bastards, to getting justice for Mom. To winning.

"A pity the three of us won't be working together, Doctor. We would have had so much fun," he says with a throaty laugh. "I'll ask you once again, any last words?"

My downcast eyes scan the floor, searching for anything useful. They find nothing. My gaze meets Kennedy's. There must be some way out, some trick we can use?

My face lights up. We have one last hope. I just need to alert Kennedy. I arch my eyebrows for him, direct his eyes with mine to my right arm as I straighten it then speak the faithful words, "Some things are better left unsaid."

Recognition shimmers in Kennedy's eyes. I work my sleeve as the boss addresses Kevin.

"Place your gun on the floor carefully and kick it away, Detective. Good, that's it.... Oh, and let's not forget about Frank's gun," the boss says in a haughty voice, "slide it over to me."

Kennedy bends forward, goes down on one knee. He places Frank's gun on the floor as I free our last hope from the compartment in my sleeve. I give Kev a quick nod.

"That's it, Detective,...

The gun glides across the floor until it reaches The Facilitator. He laughs as he bends down to pick it up. "You may want to say a prayer while you're down there, Detective."

I smile at Kev, then swing my right hand backward, driving the scalpel's blade into the boss' right thigh.

"Aaargghh!" Pain dissolves his grip on me. I thrust my left elbow into his solar plexus and pull my blade from his thigh. I spin around, and in an instant, I'm on top of him. His right arm is a blur as he recovers, grabs his blade, and drives it into my chest. Shock engulfs my face as he throws me onto my back and straddles my chest. Kennedy scrambles after his gun. My arms go limp at my sides. The boss places both his hands on the blade's base. In an instant, he will drive his weight forward onto the blade, burying it in my chest. He gathers himself to thrust forward. "And now it is done." My left arm rips through the air, striking his head, knocking him off to the side of me. I press my advantage before the moment is lost, straddling him. I am dazed, disoriented from the struggle. My head is spinning. His blade hangs from my chest. I stare down at the bastard who killed my mother, the ringleader of a sick group murdering the defenseless for profit. My thoughts and anger coalesce as my left hand grabs his throat just above his voice box. My right hand presses the scalpel against his left carotid artery. Blood trickles from the skin around my blade. His left hand blindly jabs at the floor, searching for his knife, which lies just out of reach. His eyes bulge in shock and fear. I smile and look over at his knife, kicking it away.

Kennedy stands poised, his gun now secured. He starts to speak, then stops. This wretched criminal's fate is quite literally in my hands.

My baser emotions rule me, screaming out for vengeance. My grip tightens around his neck, choking the air out of him. I could drop the blade and suffocate him with both hands. Or I could thrust my scalpel into his carotid, smothering him with his own blood while he bleeds out. An agonizing death is what this low-life deserves. No one can blame me for what drives me now, for what I am about to do.

No one except the one who matters most at this moment – Ma.

I ease my grip on his throat, calling out to Kennedy with a jerk of my head. Kennedy rushes over. I climb off the criminal as Kennedy flips the degenerate, gasping for air, onto his back and cuffs him.

"You did the right thing, Chris. I'm proud of you."

Overcome with emotion, tears fill my eyes. "Thanks for letting me decide."

I look down at my chest, bewildered. How am I still alive after taking such a blow?

I smile as my hands uncover the answer.

Suspended from my neck, torn almost in two by

the blade buried in it, hangs my St. Jude medallion. I grab the blade's hilt with one hand, the medallion with the other. The blade stays buried as I strain against it. Kev puts his hand on mine. "Let me help you with that." He smiles as we free the blade from the medallion. A stream of blood runs down my chest where the blade's tip had just barely broken through my skin. I lift the medallion to my face and kiss it, remembering Mom's words when she gave it to me: "...always do good in the world...help and protect those in need, no matter how lost or hopeless their cause seems to be. Do this and St. Jude and I will always be there to protect you."

§

The police rush in. They were keeping tabs on Kennedy and me, under orders from Kelly not to intervene until Kev radioed them. They grab the degenerate boss and put him with Damples, who they apprehended earlier as he fled the scene.

I approach the crate where the banging came from. The distraction it provided allowed Kennedy and me to fight back, to turn the tide.

"Anyone in there?" I yell. Silence. I bang on the crate and repeat my question. Nothing. Then a light tapping and whimper in reply. I find the crate's latches and flip them open. Out tumbles a wrinkled, gray-haired woman, gagged and bound. We free her. Her face is flushed and hot to the touch. Barely conscious, she speaks in a whisper. "Thank you...didn't think anyone heard me." Her eyes find mine. She smiles weakly. "...were going to kill me. Banged with my head for help."

I smile at the elderly woman, overcome with joy that we saved her. "I'm Doctor Ravello. This is my partner, Detective Kevin Kennedy. Everything is going to be all right, ma'am."

§

The uniformed police file out. Two EMT's tend to the elderly woman as she slips in and out of consciousness. Several other ambulance workers care for the four other survivors – all unconscious – we freed from the crates. Each victim has the same telltale, tiny puncture mark that mom had just after her attack. The NYPD's Crime Scene Unit, CSU, begins its tasks as Commissioner Kelly offers Kennedy and me begrudging congratulations. "Certainly not how I would have drawn up the plan to apprehend these criminals." He smiles. "But you two got the job done." He turns to me, holding up a baggie with my scalpel in it. "You've got excellent instincts, Doctor Ravello, though your choice of weapons, a scalpel versus a .38 caliber revolver and a steel knife, leaves a lot to be desired." The commissioner chuckles. "Time in the police academy ought to hone those instincts, teach you the skills and protocols you need to be a good detective." He places his hand on my shoulder as he turns serious. "We'd love to have you run the DMC for us, but it's got to be your choice, son, not something the governor forces upon you. Take some time, discuss it with your family, and let us know what you decide."

"Thank you, sir, that's exactly what I'll do."

▷ Chapter 27 ◁

It's two a.m. before the dust settles. Dad, Michelle, Kennedy, and I are gathered in the living room, savoring our victory.

"You two would have been real proud of Chris," Kennedy says with a broad, appreciative smile. Michelle and Dad look on, a mix of concern and relief written on their faces. Wrapping his massive arm around my shoulder, Kennedy pulls me into a side hug. "I thought we were goners till he did this doctor-gone-mad thing with a scalpel." A self-conscious, awkward smile takes over my face. There goes my chance to downplay this whole thing.

Michelle and Dad look at each other, bewildered. "What were you doing with a scalpel at a crime scene, honey?"

I stumble through my reply. "Well, it wasn't a crime scene at that point. We were just trying to get

160

info on the guys who killed Ma." I look at Michelle and Dad, a sheepish grin spreading across my face. "And a scalpel is the closest thing I own to a weapon."

Dad pipes in. "You guys were crazy going into that situation without backup. You could have, probably should have, been killed. What the hell were you thinking? Especially you Kev, as a detective, you should know better."

"It wasn't like that, Bill. Commissioner Kelly knew what we were up to and was monitoring the situation. He had the place surrounded after we got there. I was under orders to find out what these guys were up to first, then call for backup. I was just about to signal them to come in, but that's when Chris and I were captured." I cringe during Kev's reply. He's speaking the truth, but it doesn't seem to be helping our cause.

"Yeah, what was the signal gonna be, Detective? Gun shots to your and Chris' head, for Christ sake?" Dad says with a vicious shake of his head.

Michelle puts her arms around me and locks into my eyes. "I was out of my mind with worry. Thank God you're all right! No more crazy heroics from now on! Promise me, Chris, okay?"

Dad nods in agreement. "I second that. Leave the police work to the police, Chris. You've got a medical practice to get back to."

I look at Dad, warily.

"What?! After this crazy stunt, you're not still

thinking about running the DMC for them, are you?!" he says with exasperation.

Michelle peels off of me and tilts her head at Dad and gives him the 'Now what did we talk about?' look I know all too well.

Frustrated, Dad begins to speak, then relents. Kennedy steps in. "Uh, Bill, it's pretty late. Why don't we take off, give Michelle and Chris some alone time?"

Dad grumbles his assent and the four of us exchange hugs before they leave.

Michelle and I stare at each other in silence. The big fight, my near deadly experience at the warehouse; we'll remember this night for as long as we live.

I start to speak, "Baby, I'm so sorry about everything, I–" but Michelle cuts me off.

"Me too, honey. I shouldn't have gone so crazy before, especially with Christine around. That's not like me." She bows her head as tears drip down her cheeks. "I know you're going through a lot, trying to find your way through this nightmare." She raises her head, love filling her eyes. "I'm going to do whatever it takes to help you pull through this."

I smile through my own tears. "I know you will, baby. You're my rock." I lean in and kiss her tenderly, then hug her for an eternity.

I pull back and smile at Michelle again, then turn serious. "Tonight was a big step for me. I was on top of the guy responsible for killing Ma. I had one hand wrapped around his throat, the other pressing a scalpel into his carotid artery. I was ready to have my revenge, to finish him off and be done with it." I look out our living room window at the Long Island Sound, the moon's reflection bathing in its still waters. Emotions rumbling through me, I look back at Michelle. "But in that moment I realized killing him wasn't what I wanted, wasn't what you or Ma would want me to do either." I reach around my neck and take off the fractured St. Jude medallion, showing it to Michelle before I place it in her hands and wrap mine around hers.

"Nothing will ever bring Ma back, and I don't know if I can ever really get closure about her death, but I have to try...for you, the kids, and myself. I have to live my life so I honor Mom's life and memory, make the world a better place. I'm not sure what that means yet. But tonight Kev and I put a stop to a crime ring that took Ma and many others from their loved ones. It felt like a step in the right direction."

Michelle smiles. "I'm so proud of you, Chris. You made the right choice tonight – for all of us."

I smile back at her. "Thanks, babe. But what do I do? Running the DMC feels like the right move for me. I can use my medical knowledge to help save others in ways I never could as a doctor. But making that choice, well, there's a heavy price to pay for it." I look around the living room, admiring our beautiful home. "As a cop, I'll never be able to give you all this. We'd have to say goodbye to our dream house, goodbye to so many wonderful things." I exhale. It's painful for me to even speak about these things. "You and the kids deserve better than what I could provide as a detective."

"Chris, you are such an amazing husband and father. You're all the kids and I want and need." She places her hand on my cheek. "I know we'd be under a lot of stress, financially, emotionally, if you take the job. But we'll get through it; we'll find a way." She kisses me and then slides the medallion into my hands. "Why don't you tuck that away in a drawer for safekeeping?" Michelle's smile fills me with warmth and confidence. "Honey, know that whatever you choose, you'll have our full love and support."

▷ Chapter 28 ◁

Sitting in the O'Toole conference room at One Police Plaza I am relaxed, at peace with myself for the first time since Ma's death. Gone are all the struggles to save Mom, catch her killers, and find my path again in life. In their place is a deep sense of satisfaction about a job well done, about a decision made with care and conscience. For the past few weeks, I was a mess as my head and my heart battled it out. But that's over now.

Spatick, Kelly, and Blumenthal engage in idle chatter across from me. Behind me is the worse few weeks of my life. Ahead of me, I hope, a path to honor and salvation, to turning a terrible wrong into a watershed moment in my life.

Spatick looks to his left and right. "Well, gentlemen, let's get started."

He is different today, for some reason. Gone are his trademark smugness and condescension. In their absence he appears humble, vulnerable perhaps. An act for my benefit? Attempting to be more likable to sway my decision? I mull these thoughts over as his eyes lock in on mine.

"Doctor Ravello, this city owes you an immense debt of gratitude. Spurred on by your mother's senseless attack and murder, you accomplished in one night what the NYPD could not do for the last three months. Namely, you identified and apprehended one of the key players in a crime ring that preyed on this city's most vulnerable citizens." Spatick nods to his right at John Kelly. "As we speak, Commissioner Kelly's men, along with the district attorney, are recording confessions which will be instrumental in prosecuting the leaders of this ring." Spatick rises up and extends his hand across the table as Blumenthal and Kelly smile and clap. "We offer our deepest thanks to you on a job well done."

I rise up, my hand meeting his as I smile and nod at everyone. "Thank you very much, Governor, Commissioner Kelly, Mayor Blumenthal. I was happy to be of service, and thank you for allowing me to unofficially pursue my mother's attackers. It means a lot to me."

Spatick's smile disappears. "It's unfortunate we can't credit you with the arrest, Doctor. That will have to go to the officers who initially identified Gonzalez and Damples. Nonetheless, your and Detective Kennedy's

166

work on this case was outstanding." Spatick looks over to Kelly again, his earlier benevolence gone. He shakes his head. "Our own DMC hadn't even identified this crime ring as medical in nature. It was being investigated by the Missing Persons squad instead." Kelly winces as Spatick continues, "Imagine that; rampant trafficking of human organs taking place right under the DMC's collective noses."

"Doctor Ravello, it's painfully obvious the DMC, NYPD, and most important of all, the citizens of New York State are in desperate need of your services. I don't want to be heavy handed about this." Spatick looks again to his right and his left. "Mayor Blumenthal, Commissioner Kelly, and I understand this decision has tremendous consequences for you and your family. You'd be taking a big pay cut to join a struggling unit at NYPD. The DMC, due to its poor track record, has lost the luxury of time. You'll need to turn it around quickly or risk its collapse and dissolution." Spatick comes up for air, adjusts his tie, and continues his barrage. "The hours will be long, the stress severe, and the danger immense. We understand all of this, and so the decision must be yours, not one we force on you."

I swallow hard and twist my head, relieving the tension in my neck. "Well, no one can accuse you of giving me the hard sell, Governor," I say with a wry smile that dissolves before I continue. "In defense of the DMC, sir, there's a lot about this organ trafficking scheme that doesn't add up. Why take older people's organs instead of acquiring younger, healthier ones? How can the attacks be random when donors and recipients need to be checked for tissue compatibility? Why did all of the victims have a diamond-shaped set of small punctures on their neck? I can see why nobody connected the dots on this one. Frankly, I feel luck, not great detective work, is responsible for our success on this case."

Spatick stares at me, disbelief morphing into confusion. Self-effacing honesty and cutting others slack are foreign to him. In time a smile spreads across his face. "I appreciate your candor, insightfulness, and modesty, Doctor Ravello, not to mention your defense of the DMC. But, you still haven't answered the question that brought you here today. Will you come on board and run the DMC for us?"

I smile back at Spatick, my expression belying the thoughts running through my head. Detective work is difficult and demanding. It's thankless under the best of circumstances. The task that lies before me is incredibly challenging: run a fledgling division of NYPD straight out of the police academy while a prickly governor looks over my shoulder. But I'm not deterred. The DMC needs me...almost as badly as I need them.

"It'll be my pleasure gentlemen. How soon can I start?"

▶ Chapter 29 ◀

Iscratch my head as I pull the Firebird into my driveway behind Dad's car. Did I forget we were supposed to meet? Life has been so crazy lately, anything is possible.

I rap on Dad's car window. Startled, he looks up at me, then opens the door as I back away. "Hey, Dad, my bad. Have you been here long?"

"Sorry to drop by unexpectedly, Son. No, I just got here a minute ago." Dad looks at me pensively. "I didn't like how we left off the other day. Can I come in?"

"Oh, sure." I wave him on, then head towards the door with him. I fumble with my keys as we reach the big brown WELCOME mat perched on our stoop. Dad puts his hand on mine, quieting my movement.

"Look, let me just get right to it. I should never have come down on you and Kennedy so hard." Dad's eyes meet mine. Discomfort is written across his aged face.

"I just don't want to see either of you hurt. Working as a detective all those years, I know how dangerous the job can be."

"I understand, Dad. Sorry I had you and Michelle worried so much." I consider saying more but hold off. Dad looks like a man only halfway through what he needs to say.

"Chris, you're a grown man. You can make your own decisions." He looks at the face of our expansive home then back at me. "You and Michelle have a great life here, one I wouldn't want to see you give up. But, it's not up to me; it's up to you and Michelle to decide."

"Decide what?" Dad and I turn, startled, as the front door opens and we see Michelle standing there.

Dad looks at Michelle, then me, a lost little boy unsure which path to take. He reaches out, touches Michelle's forearm as we enter the house.

"I don't know what you two have discussed regarding Chris' work decision, and I don't want to influence you in any way..."

Michelle and I look at each other quizzically, then back to Dad.

He looks at the floor, then back up. "Well, what I'm trying to say is this: I know I came across as pretty negative the other day on Chris becoming a detective." Michelle and I stiffen. "I, well, I don't want to push you towards or away from that now. But I want to throw in my support if that's what you both decide." Dad looks past the foyer towards the grand staircase, then back to us. "You're gonna need a different house in a more affordable neighborhood if you make the change." A big smile fills Dad's face as we hold our collective breaths. Where is this monolog going? "I've got an investment house I picked up in Peekskill. The area's nothing like this, but it's yours if you'd like it." His eyebrows rise. "It's like the house our family first moved to in Ossining."

Michelle and I relax, smiling. "That's so nice of you, Bill," Michelle says with sincerity.

"Yes, Dad, that's very generous of you. I'm not sure what to say. I just got back from my meeting downtown with the governor, police commissioner, and mayor." I look at my wife. "Michelle and I were about to talk things over."

"Uh, okay. Sorry to intrude," he stammers. "Let me get out of your hair." He looks at Michelle and me, his face a mixture of love and sadness. "Whatever you two decide I'm one hundred percent behind you, okay?"

Michelle and I smile back at him. We hug him and thank him for his support. "I'll call you later, Dad." I close the door behind him and turn back to Michelle.

"Well, that was unexpected," I say.

"Aw, your dad is so sweet to offer us the house. I feel so bad for him. I wish there was some way we could help him."

I rub the back of my neck. "Me too, honey. It's

been such an intense few weeks for all of us." I wrap my arms around Michelle, nestling her head in my chest, enjoying the warmth of her body against mine.

I savor these quiet moments with Michelle. They have been all too rare of late. The upheaval of my career change will make them even rarer.

Michelle leans back, her gaze filled with serenity, acceptance – and love. "He's right, you know?"

"Who?"

"Your father." Michelle cradles my face in her hands. The love in her eyes overwhelms me. "We will need a different place to live." I'm humbled by her selflessness. Tears fill my eyes.

"You knew?"

She nods. Tears of joy fill her eyes.

"How?"

Her right hand slides down my face and neck, coming to rest over my heart.

"You're too good a man to decide differently." Tears of joy stream down our faces. "And I love you so much because of it." Michelle's face rises up to meet mine. We kiss tenderly, our wordless lips saying so much.

There was no way to know the challenges, the turmoil that lay ahead for us. But for now, we bask in the glory of our love for each other, knowing we can face any obstacle, any tragedy – together.

Acknowledgments

Heartfelt thanks to Eilene, whose love and tireless support mean so much to me personally and professionally.

My deepest appreciation goes out to Penny, Tristan, and Phyllis. You are my trusted and insightful beta readers. I thank you for taking the time to help shape this work.

Congrats to Christine Keleny for her excellent formatting and editorial work and to Anne Pottinger and Diana Delfino for their meticulous proofreading.

As always, many thanks to Diane and Jimmy. You light up my life and fill me with inspiration and happiness.

Finally, thanks to Eilene and Diane for their help with designing the cover, and to Jim Kukral at authormarketingclub.com for his tireless work doing multiple cover design revisions.

About The Author

William Rubin is a practicing physician who enjoys weaving tales of medical/scientific intrigue. Writing for him is equal parts catharsis, creativity, and escape from the rigors of a busy medical practice and the joys and challenges of raising a family.

The works of James Patterson, Robin Cook, Michael Palmer, and Patricia Cornwell inspired Dr. Rubin to create the Chris Ravello Medical Thriller Series. The first book released in the series, *Forbidden Birth*, has enjoyed a place on the Amazon Best Sellers lists for Medical Thrillers and Medical Fiction since January 2017.

Challenges and tragedies in Dr. Rubin's life, particularly the untimely death of his mother, provided some of the underlying drama, conflict, and turmoil for the series' lead character.

When he isn't busy practicing medicine or crafting his next medical thriller, Dr. Rubin enjoys time with his family and friends, running, playing piano, and traveling.

To find out more about William and what is

coming next for Chris Ravello, visit the author's website: werubin.wordpress.com, or Facebook: william.erubin. You can connect with William on Twitter @ werubin671, or Goodreads. You can also email him and/or have your name added to his growing e-mail list at werubin67@gmail.com.

William values your thoughts, insights, and feelings on *Forbidden Beginnings: Jacqueline's Tragedy,* so please post a review on your favorite websites/blogs.

Discussion Guide

1) What are the main themes in *Forbidden Beginnings: Jacqueline's Tragedy*?

2) Are you satisfied with how Dr. Rubin handled Chris Ravello's desire for vengeance and justice?

3) By the end of the book, what do you think Chris learned about himself and how to handle his mother's death?

4) Which characters would you like to learn more about in future stories?

5) What were your favorite parts of this book and why?

6) How do you feel about the emotional journey Dr. Ravello took in this book?

7) What are your thoughts about Chris' decision to leave behind his medical practice to work as a detective/lead investigator for the Division of Medical Crimes? Given similar circumstances, would you have made the same choices? Why or why not?

Keep reading for a sneak peek at the next
Chris Ravello Medical Thriller.

FORBIDDEN
BIRTH

⊳ Chapter 1 ⊲

New York City, April 2015

The killer obliterated the young woman's body. Long smooth strokes alternated with short vicious ones, tearing apart the woman's abdomen as she lay motionless before him. Reflections danced off the polished instrument in his hand as it sliced through the air, blood dripped off the blade. Oh, how he reveled in it! His prize now in closer proximity, he slowed his work, delighting in the control and skill he had acquired from years of practice and careful study.

"What a shame it has taken me so long to find my true calling," he said to himself as he thrust fourteen feet of coiled, glistening intestines out of his way. "But this is it! This is my life's work."

A few key cuts and he had what he had been searching for in the palm of his hand. He pulled it out and examined its symmetry, its beauty, its potential.

For some time now, he had decided who lived

and who died—and who would be born again. He had built up this state-of-the-art lab from nothing over the last six and a half years. His clientele now included the wealthiest, most powerful people in the world. He produced high-priced miracles for them and they, in turn, unwittingly funded all he had worked so hard to create. After years of toiling in secrecy, the time had come to reveal himself. The world would learn of his intelligence and power. The world would learn to fear and respect The Giver, the moniker he had chosen for himself.

He looked up from the mangled corpse that lay before him and turned his attention to the flat screen monitor a few feet away. It was an NBC special report that he didn't want to miss. New York State Governor Gregory Spatick was answering questions from a well-dressed reporter who sat across from him.

"Governor, you've allocated a great deal of time, money, and manpower to your pet project, the Division of Medical Crimes. To date, they have not solved a single crime. Aren't you concerned the federal government will withhold funding, shuttering the unit, if the DMC continues to fail?"

Spatick uncrossed his legs, shifted in his chair, and tentatively re-crossed his legs. "Janet, we have wonderful news to report for the DMC. Doctor Chris Ravello has just been appointed the lead detective for the Division of Medical Crimes...

"Governor, it's unheard of for an NYPD officer to become a detective after only two months on the job. With such limited experience, what qualifies Detective Ravello to now become the DMC's lead investigator?" the blond said with a furrowing of her brow.

"Chris Ravello is the only physician-detective in the NYPD history. Doctor Ravello brings experience, knowledge, and a unique perspective to the fight against medical crimes in New York. I wholeheartedly believe the DMC will flourish under Detective Ravello."...

Hands still and folded in front of him, The Giver smiled to himself as the television droned on. Not only had the dead woman in front of him given him *exactly* what he needed, she was his perfect calling card. Her appearance would jolt Ravello. Indeed, it would disturb him to his core.

"Ravello is doomed to failure, just like all those before him. They haven't caught me yet and bringing on that punk doctor won't help," The Giver said with a laugh "They don't realize how powerful and dangerous I am, but Ravello will soon find out."

The Giver closed the Styrofoam container labeled Organ Tissue Donor. This would hold his specimen, preserving and protecting the next link in what he saw as a brilliant plan. It would also deflect any prying questions from those who worked in the lab but were not yet privy to The Giver's plans. He meticulously cleaned his instruments and put them away for later use. Next, he wrapped the body and cleaned every surface so that no one else would suspect where the tissue had come from. He then crammed the body into a large plastic container, dropped down the lid, placed it on a wheeled cart, and rolled it out the door. *Soon Ravello will find this body in one of New York City's landmark locations, and that's when the fun will begin.*

Before he turned off the lights, he inspected the room one last time.

"They have no clue who or what they are dealing with. And they never will."